# The Fling

# The Fling

## John R. Erickson

Illustrations by Gerald L. Holmes

Viking

VIKING
Published by the Penguin Group
Penguin Putnam Books for Young Readers,
345 Hudson Street, New York, New York 10014, U.S.A.
Penguin Books Ltd, 27 Wrights Lane, London W8 5TZ, England
Penguin Books Australia Ltd, Ringwood, Victoria, Australia
Penguin Books Canada Ltd, 10 Alcorn Avenue, Toronto, Ontario, Canada M4V 3B2
Penguin Books (N.Z.) Ltd, 182-190 Wairau Road, Auckland 10, New Zealand

Penguin Books Ltd, Registered Offices: Harmondsworth, Middlesex, England

Published simultaneously by Viking and Puffin Books, divisions
of Penguin Putnam Books for Young Readers, 2001

1 3 5 7 9 10 8 6 4 2

LIBRARY OF CONGRESS CATALOGING-IN-PUBLICATION DATA
Erickson, John R., date
The fling / John R. Erickson ; illustrations by Gerald L. Holmes
p. cm. – (Hank the cowdog ; 38)
Summary: Abandoned and lost in a strange town, Hank the Cowdog,
law-abiding head of ranch security, embarks on a spree of fun and mischief
with a jailhouse mutt named Ralph.
ISBN 0-14-131174-6
[1. Dogs—Fiction. 2. Ranch life—West (U.S.)—Fiction.
3. West (U.S.)—Fiction 4. Humorous stories.] I. Holmes, Gerald L., ill. II. Title
PZ7.E72556 Fl 2001 [Fic]—dc21 00-068411


Viking ISBN 0-670-89640-3

Hank the Cowdog® is a registered trademark of John R. Erickson.

Printed in the United States of America
Set in New Century Schoolbook

*This book is dedicated to Larry Shire and Karen Gottlieb, valued friends of Hank.*

# CONTENTS

# CHAPTER ONE

# Cows in My Office

It's me again, Hank the Cowdog. Here's a question: What would a dog do if he suddenly found himself in town, lost and abandoned and twenty-five miles from home?

A lot of your ordinary mutts would sit down and bawl. That's what Drover would do, sit down and bawl and moan about his so-called bad leg. Not me. What I would do is what I did: go out on a wild fling in town, beat up all the local thugs, and then hike all the way back to the ranch—braving buzzards, howling winds, and bloodthirsty coyotes.

Pretty impressive, huh? Well, that's what I did.

See, I've always had a taste for adventure. Some dogs don't. They're content to lie around on the porch and snap at flies. That can get pretty

1

boring. Furthermore, we dogs aren't allowed in Sally May's yard, much less on her front porch, so you can see right away that sitting around on the porch and snapping at flies was never much of an option for me.

Anyways, it all began one morning in August, as I recall, yes it was, because it was still summer and . . .

Hmmm. At this very moment, even as we speak, a fly is crawling around on my nose. It tickles. I can't go on until I do something about this. Hang on whilst I go into Fly Countermeasures.

Fly Countermeasures aren't the same as Flea Countermeasures. Did you know that? Maybe not. With fleas, we go into a Digging and Hacking

Routine with one of our powerful hind legs, which of course is very strenuous. With flies, we merely watch the hateful little things buzz around our face until one of 'em gets careless, and then . . .

Wait. Watch this.

SNAP!

Got him, blew him right out of the sky! Heh heh. Say good-bye to another tormenting fly.

Okay, back to work. Where were we? We were discussing . . . I don't remember.

It'll come to me in a second.

Be patient. I've contacted Data Control. They're working on it.

We've had some nice sunsets lately, haven't we? Oh, and did you hear . . .

*Ralph!* That's what we were talking about. Okay, now we're cooking.

You remember Dogpound Ralph? Basset hound, long ears, sad eyes, drooping face. He lived at the Twitchell dog pound and we'd been pals for a long time. Well, who'd have thought that old slow-talking, slow-walking Ralph would run away from the dogcatcher and . . .

We weren't talking about Ralph. That comes later, but you're not supposed to know, so forget that I said anything about Ralph. In fact, I didn't. I said nothing, almost nothing at all, about Ralph.

It was August on the ranch. It was August everywhere in the world. I awoke around dawn, which means that I had caught a few winks of sleep on my gunnysack bed.

Have I mentioned that I'm Head of Ranch Security? I am, and it's a grueling job—eighteen hours a day, sometimes twenty or even thirty. Hour after hour of patrolling headquarters, chasing monsters out of the bushes, barking at smart-aleck birds and passing airplanes, barking up the sun every morning, humbling the local cat, you name it.

On and on, the work never ends, and sometimes I have to go days, weeks, even months without sleep. Okay, I don't suppose I've ever gone months without sleep . . . or even weeks, but days, yes. Sometimes I go days without . . . okay, except for naps. I grab a nap when I can, but you get the picture.

*This is a very tough job.* It's a killer. No ordinary dog could take it. But I am no ordinary dog.

Anyways, I had managed to finish up the night's patrol work around two A.M. Confident that my ranch would make it through another night, I returned, exhausted, to my office/bedroom beneath the gas tanks.

Drover was already there, of course. He's always there, growing roots in his gunnysack bed and

4

sleeping his life away. He was making his usual orchestra of odd sounds: grunting, wheezing, yipping, snoring. He does all that stuff in his sleep. Sometimes I just sit there and listen, and marvel at all the weird noises he makes.

I listened to him for a while, then tried to force my body to relax. Some dogs can do that, you know, impose stern mental discipline upon their bodily parts and force them to relax. That's what I needed, to relax and rewind. Unwind.

I couldn't do it. I tried, but my body was as tense as molten steel and my mind was racing along at a hundred miles an hour. I tried everything. I stared at the moon, listened to the night birds, took deep breaths, and even counted sheep, which is tricky on a cattle ranch. We have no sheep, don't you see.

Nothing helped. I was wide awerp and there was no chunk that I would be able to snerp. No, I would just hack to sit there, bonking the honking . . . snork murk sizzle . . .

Okay, so maybe I drifted off at last. Who wouldn't have drifted off? I was beat, bushed, exhausted, and the next thing I knew . . .

HUH?

I heard cattle, a whole herd of . . . I hearded cattle, a whole . . .

Let's back off and try that again. Suddenly my ears picked up the sounds of approaching cattle. Hundreds of 'em, thousands of 'em. They were mooing and bawling, and I could hear the thunder of their hooves on the ground.

Perhaps this was a dream. Yes, surely it was. I was dreaming that I had just taken the job as U.S. Marshal in Dodge City, Kansas. The local citizenry had finally gotten fed up with lawlessness and insolent cats, and they had begged me to take the marshal's job and clean up the town.

And now, what was this? Somebody was driving a herd of cattle right down the middle of Main Street? Not only that, but some of the dingbat cows had just walked into my office!

I raised my head and cracked open both eyes. I found myself staring straight into the eyes of thirty-seven thousand cows.

I lifted my eyes and narrowed my lips. Wait. I narrowed my eyes and lifted my lips, there we go, and initiated a deep rumbling growl in the throat-alary region of my throat.

"Get out of my office, you brainless spuds, or I'll hang the whole lot of you."

One of them, a red baldface, had the nerve to extend his neck and stick his nose right in my face. He sniffed me. Was I going to sit there and take

that? A sniffing? In my own office? I, the U.S.
Marshal of . . .

Huh?

I blinked my eyes several times. My gaze
swept the surrounding countryside, and suddenly
it struck me that . . . uh . . . this wasn't Dodge City.
It was the ranch—*my* ranch. Perhaps I had dozed,

yes, finally sleep had chased me down and captured me for a few moments of healing slumber. In other words, I was no longer marshal of Dodge City, and therefore my office was not being invaded by a herd of unruly cows. I blinked again, and waited for the cows to disappear. They didn't. I poked myself to be sure I wasn't still dreaming. I wasn't, so what were all these cows doing...

"Drover, wake up, Code Three! We've got cows in the office!"

It was true. The cow herd that usually stayed in the home pasture now had our office surrounded, and some had even wandered inside.

Drover's head shot up and his eyes popped open. They were crooked, and so were his ears. He stared into the faces of the invading multitudes. After taking one look, he just...vanished. I mean, one second he was there, and the next he was gone. ZOOM! I don't know where he went. The machine shed, most likely. That was his usual hiding place when he felt the need to flee from Reality as It Really Is.

So there I was, alone, one against thirty-seven thousand trespassing cows. Was I scared? Maybe, a little. Okay, I was scared, sure I was scared, and who wouldn't have been scared? If you woke up and found a hundred and thirty-seven thousand crazed bovines in your office, wouldn't you be scared?

But I didn't run, that's the important point. No sir, I did what any true red-blooded, top-of-the-line American cowdog would have done. I started snapping at noses and went straight into a barking routine that we call Full Air Horns.

Heh, heh. That got their attention, the little dummies, only they weren't so little. In fact, they were huge dummies, but it got their attention. They shrank back from the piercing blare of my Full Air Horns, formed a half-circle, and stared at me.

I pulled myself up to my full height of massiveness. I had 'em going now. "Okay, darlings, I'll make this brief. You came into my office without knocking and you've disturbed my sleep. I don't like that. Now, the next silly son of a gun who steps in here without permission will face the usual consequences. He'll walk out with no ears and tooth tracks over ninety percent of his body. Who wants a piece of that, huh? Any takers?"

You won't believe . . .

Never mind, just skip it.

Nothing happened. They all, uh, ran away. Fled in terror.

Okay, maybe they didn't, but only because they were so DUMB. How dumb would you have to be to walk right into the office of the Head of Ranch . . . well, they did, five of 'em. Walked right back into my office, after I'd warned them and told them . . .

What was I supposed to do, stand there and get squashed under the hooves of a whole herd of wandering cows? Heck no. I, uh, left the office, shall we say, and okay, let's go right to the bitter truth.

I ran. I'm not ashamed that I ran. I was glad that I ran, because if I hadn't run, I would have been trampled and possibly eaten by these huge dog-eating cows, and you wouldn't have any more story to read.

See, I did it for YOU. Sometimes a dog has to put aside his own selfish desires and think of somebody . . .

The trouble was that I had no place to run that wasn't populated by wild crazed cows. They were everywhere! They had my office complex completely surrounded, so by George, I just lowered my head and bulled my way through the middle of 'em.

Oh, and I barked. I'll admit that it wasn't my best bark. It was one we call "Let Me Out of Here," and it was more of a squeak than my usual deep manly tone of barking, but this was an emergency situation.

When those cows saw and heard me ripping through their ranks, they bolted and ran, and suddenly I realized . . . hey, they thought I was chasing *them*! And they were scared. In other words, I had somehow managed to turn this deal around!

Yes, they ran like the cowards they really were, and once I had 'em in blind retreat, I showed no mercy. Somewhere in the back of my mind, I knew that chasing cattle was something of a No-No on our outfit, but . . .

"Hank!"

. . . I went after 'em anyway. The fools. The idiots. Did they think I was going to run from them? Ha. Little did they know . . .

"Hank! Get out of the way, you're going to cause a stampede!"

HUH? Had somebody . . .

You probably don't need to know what happened next. Besides, it's classified information.

Sorry.

# CHAPTER TWO

# Drover Wants to Be a Truck

Nothing happened. Honest.

You thought I heard a voice? Someone calling my name? It was just the, uh, call of a bird. A quail down along the creek. They chirp and twitter, you know, and make a whistling noise: "Bob-white! Bob-white!"

Who or whom is Bob White? We don't know that, and since it involves birds, we really don't care. The point is that your bobwhite quails make that sound, and it sounded a whole lot like "Hank." No kidding. And so the voice we heard . . .

Okay, might as well admit it. It wasn't a quail calling. It was Loper and Slim, the cowboys on this outfit, and the deal was . . .

Had anyone notified ME that they would be

rounding up the home pasture first thing in the morning, or shipping steers or driving them right through my office? I mean, I'm Head of Ranch Security. It's my job to schedule things and direct traffic and make sure . . .

How did they expect me to run the ranch when they planned these events without consulting me? One minute I'm catching a few moments of precious sleep, and the next thing I know, I've got a herd of cows running through my office.

Steers, actually. They were steers, not cows. Your cows are adult females who deliver baby calves, while your steers are grown calves who are ready to go to market. But the crucial detail here is that nobody bothered to inform me.

Well, I was outraged. I was furious. I had come within a gnat's eyebrow of making a complete and utter fool of myself. I mean, they were trying to pen those steers in the corral, and I was chasing them back into the pasture, so naturally . . .

They were pretty mad, the cowboys were. I can't say as I blamed 'em for being mad, but by George, it was their own fault. And after Loper had chased me up to the machine shed—and I mean he was swinging his rope and yelling and everything—after he'd chased me away from the scene of their foolish follyrot, I stuck my head out of the machine shed doors and beamed Loper and Slim Glares of Righteous Anger.

Next time, maybe they would go through the proper channels and do it right.

Well, I was in the midst of beaming microwaves of Righteous Anger at our crew of rookie cowboys, when all at once I felt that I was being watched. I turned my head and saw . . . Drover.

"Don't stare at me. I'm transmitting a very important message to the careless and misguided people who caused this mess."

"Boy, it sure looks like a wreck. Did you do all that yourself?"

"No, I did not. This is the result of poor planning and sloppy management. I had nothing to do with it."

"I'll be derned. I thought you made 'em stampede."

"That conclusion is based on gossip and faulty information, Drover."

"Yeah, that was pretty brave. I couldn't have done it myself. I'm scared of cows."

"They were steers."

"Thanks."

"You're welcome."

"I can't believe you went after 'em like that. What a hero."

14

*Hero?* I caught a glimpse of him out of the corner of my gaze. His eyes were shining with . . . well, adoration and admiration. "Well, Drover, if you must know, I had the choice of running away or making a stand."

"Yeah, and you stood up for what was right. What a guy!"

"Well, I . . . how can I say this without seeming to brag?" I began pacing back and forth in front of him, as I often do when my mind is plunged into deepest thought. "It was a clear case, Drover. The steers had made a forced entry into the office. They were trespassing. They had no right to be there."

"So you *did* run 'em off?"

I paused for a moment and turned my gaze skyward. "Yes, you're right. I didn't want to boast about it. You know how I feel about roasting and bagging . . . bagging and broasting . . . bragging and . . . it just isn't, well, my nature to thump my own tub, as they say, but . . . yes. I had to do what was right. I gave them fair warning, and when they didn't leave, I thrashed them."

"Gosh, I wish I could do things like that."

"It comes with practice, son."

He sighed. "I think it'll take more than practice for me."

I studied the runt for a moment. "Yes, I see

your point. Fear seems to be a problem for you."

"Yeah, and I'm especially scared of cows."

"Those were steers, Drover, not cows."

"Yeah, but they all look the same to me, and they all scare me."

"Drover, what you need . . ." At that very moment, my lecture was cut short by a loud roaring sound. My ears shot up. "Holy smokes, what's that?"

Drover dived back into the machine shed. "I don't know, but it's loud, and loud noises scare me."

"Drover, the problem with you is . . ." I ventured a few steps away from the door and peered off to the east. I saw the source of the loud noise and returned to the shed. "You can come out, Drover, it's only a truck."

I heard his voice coming from the far corner of the shed. "Are you sure? What kind of truck?"

"It's a . . . how should I know what kind of truck? The truck part is bright red, and it's pulling a huge trailer that's silver."

"I'll be derned. It must be a cattle truck."

"Ha. I don't think so. No, Slim and Loper would never . . ." I studied the truck again. "It's a cattle truck, Drover, and do you see what this means?"

"Yeah. It's loud, and I can't stand loud noises in the morning."

"No, that's not what it means at all. It means that Slim and Loper ordered a cattle truck without consulting me! The guy just shows up, blaring his motor and leaving tracks on my road, and nobody bothered to tell me. This is an outroge, Draver, and something must be done about it."

"Well, I'm kind of busy right now. And my name's Drover."

"Get yourself out here, and that's an order. Hurry. And by the way, I know your name." He dragged himself out of the depths of the shed and appeared at the door. "What's wrong with you? You look sick."

"No, I'm scared of red trucks."

"See? Just as I suspected. That's an irrational fear, Drover. Why should you be any more afraid of red trucks than green trucks?"

"I'm scared of green ones too."

"Have you ever seen a green cattle truck?"

"Well . . . not really."

"My point exactly. If you've never seen a green truck, then how do you know that you're scared of them? You see, green is merely a color, and it's totally irrational to be afraid of a mere color."

"Yeah, but I'm scared of big trucks, 'cause they roar and belch black smoke."

"Belching is impolite, Drover, but it's nothing

to fear. I've heard you belch before. Were you frightened by your own belching?"

"No, but I don't belch black smoke. And I'm not a truck."

I glared at the runt. "Drover, I'm aware that you're not a truck. Do you think I'm an idiot?"

"I've wondered."

"What?"

"I said . . . I'm not a truck."

"Of course you're not a truck. If you were a truck, you wouldn't be a dog, but what's wrong with being a dog? Why, all of a sudden, do you want to be a truck?"

"Well, I guess . . . boy, I sure get confused."

"Exactly my point. You're confused, Drover. Any dog who dreams of being a truck is badly confused. We need to . . ." I stopped in midsentence and walked a few steps away. "I seem to have lost the thread of this conversation. What were we discussing?"

"Well, you said I couldn't be a truck. But I already knew that, and besides, I never wanted to be a truck. I'm happy just being a dog."

I walked back over to him and looked into his eyes. "Do you really mean that? If it's true, Drover, then this conversation has had a huge impact on your life. If you feel that you can find happiness and meaning in your dogness, then this has been time well spent." His eyes crossed. "Don't cross your eyes while I'm talking to you about the meaning of life."

"Okay, sorry."

"Now, tell me the truth. Do you think you can go on with your life, even though you're not a truck?"

"I guess so."

"Great!" I whopped him on the back. "We've managed to pull you back from the edge of the brink. Now, I observe that there's an unidentified cattle truck on this ranch. Let's march down there and give him the barking he so richly deserves. Are you ready for this?"

"I'm still a bit confused."

"Get used to it, son. Some of us are born confused and some of us get that way through hard work. Now, let's move out. For this maneuver, we'll go to Turbo Four."

"I don't have a two-by-four."

"In that case, follow me and study your lessons. We're going to show this guy what happens when cattle trucks show up on our ranch without permission. Let's go!"

And with that, we taxied out of the machine shed. After a brief takeoff sequence, I rammed the throttle down and went straight into Turbo Four. Trees, rocks, and other objects flew past.

Halfway down the hill, I saw trouble looming up—
a bunch of chickens.

I barked a warning.

"Out of the way, you fools!"

I had to alter my course just a bit to run
through the middle of them, but I got 'er done and
bulldozed 'em. What fun! What joy! Their squawk-
ing and flapping brought a rush of new meaning
into my life, and once again I understood why no
ranch dog should ever wish to be a truck.

That's kind of weird, isn't it, Drover wishing
he could be a truck? Oh well. He's weird. I've said
it many times.

And so it was that Drover and I intercepted the
trespassing truck just as it was turning around
and getting ready to back up to the loading chute.
I roared up beside the cab and began laying down
a withering barrage of barking. Drover joined me
and added a yip or two.

"Halt! Stop that thing and park it, buddy. We
need to see some paperwork before you back up to
our loading chute."

The driver stared at me. Description: small
guy, young, big black cowboy hat pushed down on
his ears, glasses that made him look like a dragon-
fly, and a stringy little mustache that I would have
been ashamed to wear out in public.

He stared at me and kept backing up.

"Okay, pal, we tried it the easy way. Get out of that truck or we're fixing to disable it."

He ignored me. How foolish of him.

That left me with little choice. I rushed to the left front wheel and was just about to rip it to shreds with my enormous jaws, when . . .

HUH?

CHAPTER THREE

# We Apply the Secret Chemical Agent

**H**ang on, you won't believe this.

Suddenly the sky opened up and I was pelted with hailstones the size of geese eggs. Goose eggs, I guess it would be, the size of goose eggs, and they struck me on the head and back, causing no small amount of pain.

"Back off, Drover, we've got a hailstorm in progress! Take cover!"

We cancelled the combat mission and took cover in front of the saddle shed. There, we hunkered down and waited for the storm to pass.

I turned to Drover. "Boy, that was close."

"Yeah, the driver beaned you with a cup of ice."

"A cup of . . . don't be ridiculous, Drover. Those were huge hailstones and . . ."

I searched the sky for hail clouds. There were no clouds, none.

Laughter? Laughter from the truck? I crept out of the storm shelter and cast a glance . . .

Okay, what we had here was a childish, infantile truck driver who had . . . Have we discussed truck drivers? I don't like 'em, never have, and the very worst are the ones who drive cattle trucks. They all think they're hot stuff, see, because they sit up there in the cab of a huge truck and can look down on the rest of the world.

Well, he would pay for this. He had no idea what happens to truck drivers who throw cups of ice at the Head of Ranch Security. I had a little truck in my bug . . . a little trick in my bag, let us say, that would make him regret his foolish behavior.

I whirled around to my assistant. "Okay, Drover, this guy wants trouble, so we're fixing to give him trouble in shovels."

"Spades."

"What?"

"Trouble in spades. That's what you meant."

"That's what I said—trouble in spades."

"No, you said shovels in truffles . . . troubling shovels . . . I don't know what you said."

"If you don't know what I said, don't try to correct me. And don't forget who's in charge around here."

"Trouble in shovels."

"What?"

"That's what you said. You said 'shovels' but you meant 'spades.'"

I stuck my nose in his face. "Do we have time to argue the difference between a spade and a shovel? They both dig holes."

"No, I think spades are cards."

"On this ranch, a spade is a shovel, and that's the end of the conversation. Do you have a problem with that?"

"What about posthole diggers?"

"They're in the same category, and I'm afraid we're out of time." The truck made contact with the loading chute, and the smarty-pants driver set the air brakes. I turned to my assistant. "All right, Drover, I guess you know what comes next."

"Well, let's see. We'll sit here and watch?"

"No. We're going to put all eighteen wheels of his eighteen-wheeler on Total Lockdown, using our secret chemical agent."

"You mean . . ."

"Exactly. He'll never leave this ranch without dealing with us. You take the west side and I'll take the east."

He gulped. "All of 'em? Nine whole tires?"

"Yes, all of 'em. It'll be a challenge, but I know you can do it."

"Yeah, but . . . what if we run out of fluid? You know me. I get all excited and . . ."

"Ration it, Drover. Don't go squirting in all directions. This is an exercise in self-discipline. We've trained for it and you can do it. Are you ready?"

"I guess."

"Great. We'll regroup at the rear of the truck in two minutes and thirty seconds. Let's move out."

Keeping our bodies low to the ground, we dashed across the open piece of ground that lay between the saddle shed and the trespassing truck. When we reached the front wheels, I called a halt and looked around, just to be sure we hadn't been observed or followed.

We were clear, so I gave Drover the Coded Signals that would propel us into the next stage of the mission. I'm sorry, but I can't reveal those signals. It's extremely sensitive information, as you might expect. Why, if our codes fell into the wrong hands, every truck driver in Texas would have them, and then there's no telling what might happen.

Oh, what the heck, maybe it wouldn't hurt, but

you must promise never to reveal this information to anyone who drives a cattle truck. Promise? Okay, hang on. Here we go.

## Coded Signal Package for Operation Total Lockdown

1. Left paw makes a counterclockwise circle in the air.
2. Left eyebrow jumps up.
3. Left eye winks once.
4. Tongue darts out of mouth to the left twice.
5. Left paw returns to the ground.

## End of Top Secret Transmission

Pretty impressive, huh? You bet it was. Our enemies have never broken this particular signal package. The thing that gets 'em is that we keep going back to the *left* side, see—left paw, left eyebrow, left eye, left tongue, and left paw. They expect us to throw in some righthanded stuff, but we don't. By the time they figure out what's happening to them, we're already done with our mission and are on our way home.

So there you are, a little glimpse at our codes and signals and so forth.

Anyway, I gave the signals and we launched

the mission. As planned, Drover took the west side and I concentrated all my firepower on the east. The first three sets of wheels were pretty easy, but then came the hard part, that long sprint from the truck wheels to the back of the trailer. By that time, a guy is getting a little tired and is feeling the effects of dehydration, and of course you have to factor in the terrible emotional strain that comes with these secret operations.

I felt all of those things, and I'll even admit that in the middle of the sprint, I thought about giving up. The fatigue, the dehydration, the terrible strain were wearing me down. What kept me going was Cowdog Pride—and the bitter memory of that cup of ice.

The truck driver would pay dearly for that cup of ice.

Oh, maybe we haven't discussed what happens to these trucks when we sprinkle the tires with the Secret Chemical Agent. Heh heh. Boy, what a weapon! It eats into the steel rims and hubs and actually *dissolves the bearings*. No kidding. And guess what happens when the smart-aleck drivers try to drive off.

Heh heh. The truck won't move. That's right, it won't move. It's on Total Lockdown, and it stays that way until the driver comes to US and begs for the Neutralizing Agent. If he's properly humble and courteous and respectful, sometimes we release the truck and let him go. If the driver gets mouthy (a lot of 'em do), we just walk away and let him live with the consequences.

You know what happens then? They have to unload all the cattle and call in three big wreckers from Amarillo, and haul off the rig in three or four sections. That's pretty harsh, but these guys have to learn not to mess with the Head of Ranch Security.

Well, I was the first to finish the mission. Exhausted, burning up with thirst, and panting for breath, I leaned against a corral post and waited for my partner to come in. At last he came dragging around the rear of the truck, gasping for breath.

"I ran out of ammo on the last tire!"

"Reload and finish the job, Drover. The entire mission depends on it."

"I can't!"

"I told you to ration your fluid. What happened?"

"Well, I got so excited . . . I don't think I'd better tell you."

"Tell me, and be quick about it."

"Promise you won't get mad?"

"Tell me. Out with it."

"Oh darn. Well, I got so excited, I . . . dribbled between tires."

My eyes rolled up in my head. "How could you dribble between tires? We've worked on that, we've drilled and practiced. That's the one mistake we weren't allowed to make."

"I know, I messed up, I'm a failure. Can you finish it for me?"

I heaved a sigh. "Okay, I'll finish your job, Drover, but only because I was wise enough to hold one squirt in reserve. Remember that part of our training? Always keep a reserve squirt."

"I know, I just couldn't control myself."

"Drover, he who can't control himself has no self-control. You think about that while I finish the job."

"I'm sorry. I tried."

"I know you're sorry, and I know you tried, but you've got to learn to hold back that last squirt."

I heaved myself up to a standing position and took a big gulp of carbon dioxygen. I felt weak and a little woozy. My entire body begged for rest and restoration, but the job had to be finished. If we left that one tire untreated . . . there was no telling what might happen, but it would be bad, very bad.

I pushed Drover aside and staggered around to the west side of the trailer. Sure enough, there it was, as plain as day—a big untreated wheel. With great difficulty, I hoisted myself into the Firing Position and took careful aim.

Click.

Huh?

I relaxed for a moment, took three deeps breath . . . deep breaths, I should say, and shifted back into the Firing Position.

Click.

Suddenly I had a feeling that Drover was staring at me. "What are you staring at?"

"What happened? It didn't go off."

"We, uh, seem to have gotten a batch of faulty ammunition, Drover."

"You mean . . ."

"I mean we got a batch of faulty ammunition, and I can't be held responsible for that." I marched past him. "Just forget it, Drover. It was too much trouble anyway."

"You mean . . ."

"Yes. Hush."

And so it was that our mission to disable the trespassing truck ended in failure. But out of the rubble of the shambles, we emerged with a valuable lesson on water conservation and resource management. Hence, we had snatched a huge moral victory out of the jaws of the feet.

Defeat, it should be. Out of the jaws of defeat.

# CHAPTER FOUR

# Yipes! I Get Trapped in a Cattle Truck!

O nce we had notched up a moral victory for the ranch, in the face of incredible odds, I set out to discover what the truck was doing there. As you know, I hadn't been informed, so it was pretty important that I find out just what the heck was going on.

Creeping through the corrals and lurking behind fence posts, I was able to pick up bits and pieces of conversation, enough to establish a pattern. Loper had decided to sell this bunch of big steers at the Twitchell Livestock Auction. The truck was there to haul them into town.

Well, that made a certain amount of sense. It wasn't a bad plan and I wasn't opposed to it, but I couldn't help being a little miffed that they had made all these plans without insulting me. *Consulting* me, let us say. I mean, sometimes my schedule is flexible and sometimes it's not. When they start shuffling cattle around, I need to know about it.

Oh well. Part of a dog's job on these ranches is working behind the scenes to keep the humans from messing things up too badly. We have to let *them* take all the credit when things go smoothly, of course, but that's okay. We're not in it for the glory, but rather for the quiet satisfaction of a job well done.

So once I had figured out what they were doing, I played the part of the loyal soldier and threw myself into the work of loading the cattle. Did Drover pitch in and help? Of course not. He's afraid of being kicked. Oh well.

Have we discussed loading cattle? I'm pretty good at it. It's one of my better skills, actually, and I've got the system worked out to a science.

Here's how it goes. The truck driver hollers out the number of cattle he needs to load certain compartments in the truck: "Ten head for the front!" We sort ten head of steers into the . . .

*"Hank, get out of the gate!"*

. . . crowding pen and shut the gate. At that point, the steers have no place to go except down the alley, up the loading chute, and into the truck.

Once that compartment is filled, the driver calls out the next number: "Thirty head." This time, instead of sorting off ten head, as we did before, we sort off thirty head and . . .

*"Hank, get out of the dadgum gate!"*

. . . and shoo them into the crowding pen and go through the same process of running them down the alley and up into the truck. Good system, huh? You bet, and once they start moving down the alley, that's when a cowdog really earns his pay.

What we do is station ourselves outside the alley and coax the dumbbell steers into the truck. We do this by marching up and down the alley, darting our noses between the boards of the corral fence, and biting the steers on the flank.

If you don't know what you're doing here, it can be dangerous. Those steers will kick, you know, and those kicks on the nose can hurt. Your better grades of cowdog will take their lumps and go right on, while your lower run of mutts will do what Drover does—disappear until the work is done.

Not me. I jumped right into the middle of the action. Sure, I got my nose rattled a time or two, but the steers who did it paid a terrible price. I always get the last bite.

The best part comes when we load the last bunch. On the last bunch, I actually move inside the alley with the cattle and personally follow them up the chute and into the truck, where I stand guard at the door until the driver gets it shut. There's something kind of satisfying about standing there in the door and, you know, basking in the glory of a job well done.

Sometimes I take this opportunity to say good-bye to the cattle and wish them a safe journey.

"Well, good-bye, you morons. It was nice having you here at the ranch, but it'll be even nicer having you gone. You ate all our grass and taking care of you was a pain in the neck. Good-bye, good riddance, and don't ever come back."

Something like that. Just a few words, heh heh, to let them know . . .

SLAM!

Huh?

Someone had . . . the driver had shut . . . *Hey! Open the door!*

Wait a minute, there'd been a big . . .

I felt the truck moving. I barked the alarm but the stupid steers were bawling and carrying on, and nobody heard me. We gathered speed. We were moving past the house. Through the slats in the side of the trailer, I could see Sally May out in her yard. Little Alfred was standing beside her. They waved good-bye to the driver.

Hey! Help! I was trapped!

They didn't hear. But surely they would notice, someone would miss me, they would sense that the Head of Ranch Security had mysteriously vanished. Of course they would, and then Sally May would leap into her car and . . . no, she wouldn't do that, she wouldn't even care.

But Slim would notice. He would leap into his pickup and leave headquarters, spinning tires and throwing up gravel, and flag down the truck driver. Of course he would. It was just a matter of . . .

Time passed and nobody came. What the heck were they doing? The Head of Ranch Security had just been kidnapped and . . .

The truck went through its gears and gathered speed.

Gulk.

A feeling of panic began moving throughout my body. Holy smokes, I was locked inside a cattle truck with sixty-five head of . . . Ranch headquarters faded into the distance. So did my hopes and plans.

Slowly, I moved my gaze to the steers. They were staring at me. I swallowed hard. They seemed to be waiting for me to . . . well, say something, and perhaps to explain my presence on their, uh, truck.

"Hi. I'm the Head of Ranch Security. The, uh, owners of the ranch felt that you guys needed a . . . well, a guard, you might say, an escort to, uh, make sure you had a safe trip . . . a happy trip, a comfortable journey, so to speak. So . . . well, here I am. How's the trip so far?"

They stared at me.

"Oh, I get it. You've never been on a guarded truck before. Ha, ha. Yes, it's a little unusual, but you know, the owners felt . . . guys, they felt that you were such an extra special bunch of steers, they wanted to make sure you had a safe and pleasant trip to town. So they . . . well, they chose the Head of Ranch Security to go along. That says something right there, doesn't it?"

No response. My mouth was suddenly very dry.

"Sure it does. I mean, they could have sent some ordinary little mutt to do the job, but that's not what they did. No sir. They went straight to the top and . . . I mean, I'm a very busy dog, I had many things to do today, but when they offered me this assignment . . . hey, I *wanted* to come, because, fellas, riding to town with you is just about the . . ."

A big black white-faced steer stepped forward. "Aren't you the dog that bit me a while ago?"

"Me? Oh, I don't think so. Surely not. No."

"You stuck your head through the fence and bit me."

"No, you're thinking of . . . uh . . . Drover, the other dog. He looks a lot like me, people are always getting us confused, and yes, he's bad about . . . uh . . . biting. Bad biter. I've tried to talk to him about that, and by George, as soon as I get back to the ranch, I'll sure . . ."

"It was you, bud." The other steers nodded.

Gulp. "It was? Are you sure?"

They all nodded.

"Okay, let me explain."

"And you called us a bunch of morons, didn't you?"

"Oh no. I would never . . . Morons? Ha, ha. What an outrageous . . . No, fellas, I'm pretty sure . . ."

"It was you, bud."

Gulp. "It was?" They nodded. Yipes. My mind was racing. "Okay, fellas, just simmer down. I think I can explain everything. Honest. See . . ."

"Shaddup."

"Yes sir."

"You ever been trampled to death?"

"Uh . . . no, never have."

"You ever been used for a soccer ball and kicked from one end of a cattle truck to the other?"

"Uh . . . no sir."

"Anybody ever used your face to mop up the floor of a cattle truck?"

"I don't think so. No."

He stuck his nose right down into my face. "If I was you, I'd curl up against that door and keep my mouth shut all the way to town."

"I was just thinking about ... uh ... doing that. Great idea."

"'Cause if you don't, all those bad things could happen to you all of a sudden."

"Right. Good point. But let me hasten to add ..."

"Shaddup."

I shutted up. Shut upped. Whatevered. I curled up in a ball and huddled against the door. I could hear them muttering and laughing, like ... I don't know what. Like a bunch of pirates, a bunch of bloodthirsty pirates plotting a mutiny.

"What a jerk."

"Yeah, and he's a dumb jerk."

"Got trapped on a load of cattle. Har, har. How dumb is that?"

"That's off-the-chart dumb."

"That's cowdog-dumb. Har, har."

I listened to their mockeries and felt a growing sense of indignation. At one point I seriously considered leaping right into the middle of 'em and whipping the whole bunch, but I managed to, uh, keep control of myself and chose instead to take the Higher Road—to be a mature dog and to ignore their sticks and stones.

That was the longest ride of my life. I thought it would never end. I didn't dare sleep, and I hardly dared even to breathe. I mean, who could relax with those big lugs yucking it up and plotting meanness? Not me.

At last the truck began to slow and we coasted into town. Through the slats in the side of the truck, I was able to see cars, people, stores, Main Street. Thank goodness, we had finally made it to Twitchell!

We turned off of Main Street, went three blocks, and made another turn. We had arrived at the Twitchell Livestock Auction. As we were backing up to the loading chute, that same smart-alecky steer bent down and said, "How's the trip so far, bud?"

"Swell. Wonderful. I can't tell you how much fun this has been."

They roared and mooed with childish mocking laughter.

The door opened and I found myself staring into the astonished eyes of the driver, and at his over-sized black hat, which pushed his ears out and made him look like a monkey, and at his miserable little excuse for a mustache.

"You? What are you doing here?"

That was for me to know and for him to figure out. I shot through his legs, scrambled through the corral fence, and got the heck out of there.

# CHAPTER FIVE

# I am Arrested
# on False Charges

Boy, what an exciting escape! I got out of there just in the nickering of time, and then I went right to work, plotting my revenge on those big lugs who had . . .

Well, they hadn't actually done much of anything, except they had mocked and laughed at me, and if you're a cowdog, that's a big deal. Pride, cowdog pride. We don't take trash off the cats or the cows or the steers, and setting the record straight is pretty derned important to us.

When they came off the truck, I was waiting outside the corral to give them the full load of Score Settlers and Mockery Countermeasures. You'll be impressed by this. As each moron passed down the alley, I stuck out my tongue at him and yelled, "I should have whipped you galoots when I had the chance! And your mother was nothing but a fat cow, so there!"

Heh, heh. Boy, that ripped 'em, just tore 'em to shreds, and there wasn't a thing they could do about it, since I was outside the corral and they were inside. In the face of such wit and intelligence, all they could do was hang their heads and trot on down the alley and say to themselves, "Gosh, what a brilliant dog! He's right, we're just a bunch of big dumb galoots, and now we're sorry we said all those hateful things to him."

See? Sometimes a guy has to wait for justice, and sometimes he has to help it along its rocky path, but justice always comes.

Well, having served the Cause of Justice and having won a huge victory over the forces of brutish ignorance, I was feeling pretty proud of myself. Why not? I had earned it in a match of wits and so forth, and don't forget that I had been out-numbered sixty-five to one. So yes, I was feeling pretty . . . well, not cocky exactly, but proud and fulfilled.

Oh, and don't forget this part. I had a strong suspicion that Loper and Slim would be just as proud and fillfulled when they heard all the facts in this case—namely, that I had guarded and escorted their investment of cattle all the way to town, and had even fought off two gangs of cattle rustlers.

Did I mention that part? Maybe not, but yes, along the road, we had been jumped, attacked, and amwhacked by two gangs of bloodthirsty cattle rustlers. Ambushed. Bushwhacked. At sixty miles an hour, we shot it out, right there on the public highway. It was a close call, but I managed to disable them with bursts of High Energy Microwave Barking.

Boy, what a fight! The thunder of horses' hooves, yelling, the zing of bullets in the air, the whole nine yards of scary and exciting stuff.

So, yes, I was feeling so good about all these triumphs, I did what any normal American cowdog would have done. I marched around to the right side of the cattle truck and lobbed a load of Secret Chemical Agent into the middle of that tire Drover had missed at the ranch.

There! Now when that hateful monkey-eared little truck driver tried to pull away from the loading chute, he would find, heh heh, that all his hubs and bearings had melted down. His truck would have to be removed in parts and pieces, and the next time he felt the urge to chunk a cup of ice at a hardworking ranch dog, he would think twice about it.

With these triumphs glowing in the theater of my mind, I pranced up to the office building. See, your livestock auctions consist of a big "yard" of pens and corrals, and also a main building, inside of which they keep an office, the sale ring, and a small cafe. The sale ring is a kind of pen with bleachers on three sides, where the cattle buyers sit.

How did I know so much about livestock auctions? Hey, I was an old hand at this business. Maybe you didn't know it, but I had come here as a pup and had taken my first job at these very stockyards. That's where I met Slim Chance, but that's another story.

Where were we? Oh yes, feeling great and triumphant, I marched past the office and caught the scent of something ... hmmm, fragrant and delicious. I called a halt to my march and switched on Smelloradar. The fragrant waves seemed to be coming from ... hmmm ... several garbage barrels near the back door of the cafe.

I tossed slow glances over all shoulders and in all directions. Nobody was watching. Nobody was even close to watching, because nobody was around. Heh, heh. And nobody would ever know how those barrels got ... well, overturned, shall we say.

THUNK! THUNK!

Just as I had suspected, the barrels contained a gold mine of great stuff: cold greasy french fries, pieces of bread, bits of hamburger, and half a tuna fish sandwich. What a find! I went right to work and began eating my way through these treasures. Great stuff!

But then, all at once, I heard a roar outside the barrel and poked out my head to see . . . hmmm. It was the cattle truck, pulling away from the loading chute. It appeared that . . . okay, I figured it out. On that last wheel—remember the last wheel?—on that last wheel job, I had forgotten to properly stir and shake up the Secret Chemical Agent, and if you don't . . .

Oh well, who cared? I was knee-deep in delicious restaurant food, so I decided to let him go—this time. But if he ever . . .

HUH?

I hadn't noticed the pickup. Or the man leaning against the fender, watching me. It was a white pickup with . . . what was that thing? A wire cage in the back, it appeared, and on the side of the pickup door was written in big red letters, CITY OF TWITCHELL ANIMAL CONTROL.

Animal control? What was animal control? I'd never heard of it. I mean, what kind of animals did they have in Twitchell that needed . . .

The man was staring at me. Glaring at me, actually, and he held a lariat rope in his hands. I wondered what he had in mind . . . I mean, why would he be holding a . . .

I stopped chewing my greasy french fries. My mouth stopped in mid-chew.

Animal control? Surely that didn't mean . . . dogcatcher, did it?

Swish!

Yes, by George, it sure did, and right then I figured out why he was carrying a catch rope.

*He was the city dogcatcher and he used the rope for capturing stray dogs!*

He caught me, is how I figured it out, and I mean the guy was so fast with that rope, I never saw it coming. He really nailed me, and at that point, I had no choice but to hit Turbo Five and break the . . .

Gulk!

. . . rope, only it was stouter than you might have supposed, and I ended up lying on my back and staring up at the blue summer sky and the dogcatcher's face. He appeared to be looking down at . . . well, at ME.

He had a toothpick parked in the side of his mouth. "No collar, no tags, and tipping over trash barrels. Pooch, you're about as illegal as a dog can be, and we've got a place for mutts like you."

Hey, wait, I could explain everything. See, I wasn't a mutt. Honest. And I had come to town on a very important assignment, guarding a load of . . . and about those trash barrels, a sudden gust of wind must have . . .

SLAM!

He wasn't interested in my story, and the next thing I knew, I had been pitched into the prison cage in the back of the pickup. I was on the inside, looking out . . . at the dogcatcher and his toothpick.

He studied me with narrowed eyes. "You know, I think we've met before."

Me? Oh no, I didn't think so. See, I didn't live in Twitchell. I was from the country, a . . . uh . . . foreign country. England. Yamoslovia. One of those foreign lands. I was just visiting. On my way home. There was no way . . .

He didn't listen. He walked away, got into the pickup, and off we went. Unless I was badly mistaken, he was hauling me to the . . . gulp . . . dog pound. Prison. Devil's Island for dogs.

It was then that I noticed another dog in the cage. I hadn't seen him until that very moment. He was curled up—asleep, if you can believe that.

"Hey you, wake up. A terrible injustice is being done here. I've been arrested on false charges. I've been kidnapped and shanghaied. My rights as a dog have been trampled, and all you can do is lie there and sleep. Wake up!"

His head came up. He was . . . some kind of hound dog. A basset. Description: big baggy sad eyes, drooping jowls, front feet that pointed outward, and an incredibly long set of ears.

He stared at me, then spoke. "Did you get caught?"

"Yes, I certainly did, and this is an outrage."

"Uh-huh. That's what they all say."

"I'm a law-abiding dog. I was doing nothing, almost nothing at all, and your town dogcatcher arrested me on false and trumped-up charges."

"Uh-huh. That's what they all say."

"I demand to speak to the mayor."

"You already did."

"I did not. I had a brief, unpleasant conversation with your stupid dogcatcher, but . . ."

"The stupid dogcatcher's our mayor."

I stared at him in shock and disbelief. "How can one man be both?"

"Small town."

"Well, there's another outrage. Okay, I demand to speak to the governor."

He shrugged. "Well, there's no law against demanding, I guess."

"Is that all you can say? Listen, pal, I'm an innocent dog and . . ." I gave him a closer look. "Wait a minute. Don't I know you?"

He yawned. "Could be, don't recall. Name's Ralph."

"Yes, of course, it's all coming back to me. You're

Dogpound Ralph! You're the dogcatcher's pet. You live at the pound. Don't you remember me?"

He looked me over with those big sad eyes. "Nope."

"Of course you do. I'm Hank the Cowdog."

"Nope."

"I'm Head of Ranch Security on a huge outfit south of town."

"Nope."

"Hey Ralph, we served some time together at the dog pound. I was on Death Row and we became dear friends."

"Huh. I can't remember names, but I always forget a face. Maybe it'll come to me here in a second. Wait. Are you the soap guy?"

"Yes, that's me. I was poisoned by my enemies. They slipped a bar of deadly foaming soap into my food, and your friend the dogcatcher thought I had hydrophobia. He arrested me and hauled me off to the dog pound. Remember?"

"Okay, sure. Well, how's life been treating you?"

"How's life been . . . Hey Ralph, right this minute things aren't looking so swell. I've been arrested on false charges and I'm on my way to prison. To be honest, that worries me. It also worries me that you don't seem to be worried."

He yawned again. "You ain't the first dog in

history to get nabbed. Happens every day."

"It happens every day! Listen, Ralph, this is . . ."

"Shhhh." A pained expression came over his face, and he pushed himself up to his feet. "I just woke up. Let me think about this."

I fought back an impulse to roar at him and tell him . . . well, I'd already told him everything, so there wasn't much I could do but sit there and let him "think about it." And just in case he didn't think about it, I thought about it.

What I thought was that I was in big trouble.

# CHAPTER SIX

# Ralph and I Make a Bold Escape

I waited for Ralph to do his thinking. I figured he would be pretty slow at it, and he was. Ralph didn't get in much of a hurry for anything.

He yawned and stretched and walked around the cage, looking out. "It's kind of a warm day, ain't it?"

"Yes. It's warm and very depressing."

"Uh-huh. Days are like that sometimes."

"I suppose."

"It's getting close to fall, ain't it?"

"Uh, Ralph, I don't want to rush you . . ."

"I've always liked the fall."

"You were going to think about my problem, remember?"

"Don't rush me."

"Sorry."

Again, I waited. Ralph sat down and scratched his right ear. "Wax."

"I beg your pardon?"

He stared at me. "Wax. I get wax in my ears and it tickles sometimes."

"How interesting. So then you have to scratch, I suppose."

"Yalp. Sometimes it helps and sometimes it don't."

"Mmmm, yes." I watched as he kicked himself in the ear. "It's probably better by now."

"Nope, still tickles."

"Great." Seconds crawled by. I watched him scratch and tried to contain myself. The pickup lurched to a stop. "Uh-oh. Is this the dog pound?"

Ralph glanced around. "Nope. Coffee time. Jimmy Joe'll be here for thirty minutes. We do this every day."

Sure enough, we had pulled up in front of the Dixie Dog Cafe. The dogcatcher climbed out, stretched a kink out of his back, and went inside. My gaze drifted back to Ralph. He was still scratching his ear.

Ralph was scratching, not the dogcatcher.

"Uh, Ralph, I've always been a dog of few words."

"Good."

"But under the circumstances, I think I'll depart from tradition."

"You worry too much."

"Could we discuss my future? You said something about developing a plan, or words to that effect."

"Uh-huh. Already did."

"You already..." I stared at him. "You've already got a plan in mind?"

"Yup. A good one too."

"Ralph, I'd be the last dog in the world to doubt what you say, but I've been here in this prison cage for the last half hour and I've seen no evidence that you were thinking or planning. You've been scratching, if I may be so blunt."

He grinned. "Helps me think, scratching does."

"Good. Fine. Could we discuss your thoughts? I mean, I don't want to seem impatient or doubtful or pushy..."

He raised a paw to his lips. "Shhhh. You're starting to get on my nerves."

That was more than I could take. "I'm starting to get on your nerves? I'm sorry, pal, but shall we be frank and earnest?"

"I'm Ralph, Dogpound Ralph, and I think your name's Hank."

"I know your name and I know my name, and

you know what else? You're starting to get on MY nerves. My life is at stake here and I demand that you stop noodling around and get down to business."

"You do, huh?"

"Yes, I most certainly do."

He yawned, pushed himself up, and waddled over to the cage door. He gave it a push with his left front paw and . . . you won't believe this . . . it swung open!

My eyes darted from the door to Ralph and back to the door. "How'd you do that?"

"Gave it a shove."

"I saw that part, but how'd you know it wasn't latched? I mean, I never would have thought . . ."

"That's the problem, see. You talk all the time and don't do much thinking."

"I resent that. For your information, I don't talk all the time."

"What are you doing now?"

"I'm . . . How'd you know the door wasn't latched?"

"'Cause I pay attention. 'Cause I knew Jimmy Joe didn't lock it. You want to leave or stay?"

My gaze went to the open door. "This isn't a trick, is it? I mean, this seems too easy, Ralph, and somehow I smell a rat."

He heaved a sigh. "The door's open."

"Right, but consider this, Ralph. My background is in Security Work, and we're trained never to fall for the obvious. When something seems too good to be true . . . Hey, where are you going?"

He hopped out of the cage and trotted away.

I edged toward the door and did a rapid Sniff and Check. See, I still wasn't convinced that this wasn't some kind of setup deal, and I wanted to check it out for, well, electronic sensors, powerful energy fields, magnetic thermocouples, and the other devices that might have been installed on the door.

To my surprise, it was clean. Nothing.

I dived through the door and into Sweet Freedom, hurried away from the awful prison truck where I had been confined for weeks, and caught up with Ralph. He was walking down the middle of a side street. I fell in step beside him. For a minute or two, neither of us spoke.

"Ralph, one question. If you knew that door was unlatched, why didn't you say so?"

"Too much trouble."

"What? I thought my life was about to end, and it was too much trouble for you to tell me otherwise?"

"You're still alive, ain't you?"

"I'm still alive, but I aged several years."

"Aged beats dead."

"I won't argue that, Ralph, but . . . where are we going?"

He stopped and sat down in the middle of the street. He looked at me with his big sad eyes. "You just keep firing questions, don't you?"

"Asking questions is part of my job, Ralph. I ask questions, seek answers, and follow every clue to its . . . Where are we going?"

"I don't know where you're going, but I'm out on a fling."

"Oh? What's a fling?" I heard him heave a sigh. "Sorry, but I'm from the country. I don't know what a fling is."

"A fling's a fling."

"Great. So what is it?"

It took me a long time, but finally I managed to drag an explanation out of him. Here's what he told me.

He lived at the dog pound, remember? Only he wasn't one of the convict dogs. He was Jimmy Joe Dogcatcher's pet. Once every month or two, he got tired of living behind bars and went on a "fling," which meant that for several hours or days, he indulged himself in naughty behavior and played chase games with Jimmy Joe.

I found this strange. "Wait a minute. The dog-catcher lets you do this? He's part of the game?"

"Yup. We both get tired of the same old stuff. When business is slow, Jimmy Joe forgets to lock the door."

At that very moment, a car approached us from the west, and there we were, sitting in the middle of the street. The car screeched its brakes, swerved, honked, and zipped past us. The breeze from the car caused my ears to ripple.

"Hey Ralph, maybe we ought to get out of the middle of the street, huh?"

He grinned. "Naw. They'll swerve. They always do."

"Yeah, but what if they don't? What if . . . Wait a minute. Is this part of your fling?"

"Uh-huh. Kind of exciting, ain't it?"

"Well, I . . . I've never thought about that, Ralph, but to be real honest . . ."

Another car came along, this one from the other direction. The driver didn't see us until the last second. He hit his brakes, smoked his tires on the pavement, and brought the car to a stop just inches away from us.

Ralph's eyes brightened with . . . I don't know what. Some kind of devilish delight, I suppose, and though I had known Ralph for quite a while, I'd never seen this side of him before.

He chuckled and gave me a wink. "That was a good 'un, wasn't it?"

The driver stuck his head out the window and blew his horn. "Get out of the road, you idiots! What do you think this is, a parking lot for mutts? I'm calling the dogcatcher!"

With that, he roared away, leaving us to roast in his angry glare.

I turned back to Ralph. "That guy was pretty mad."

"Yeah, it drives 'em nuts, me sitting in the middle of the road."

"And you think this is fun, right?"

"Yup. And you know what else?"

I cast glances over my shoulders, just in case another car was coming. "No, I don't know what else. What else?"

His eyes, usually so sad and dull, were sparkling. "There's funner stuff yet to come. The Fling has started. Jimmy Joe'll be after us any minute now."

I moved myself out of the road and sat down on the curb. "In that case, I'll be leaving soon. To be perfectly honest, I think this is a little . . . weird." Another car zoomed past, missing Ralph by inches. "Ralph, you're going to get smashed. What's the point of all this?"

He joined me at the curb, his ears dragging the ground and his toenails clicking on the pavement. "The point is that I get tired of being a good dog, so I bust out and do naughty things. Don't you ever wish you could be naughty?"

"No. I guess we're different, Ralph. You're just a jailhouse mutt. Me, I'm Head of Ranch Security."

"Uh-huh."

"It's a very heavy responsibility."

"Yalp. So you don't want to go with me and be naughty?"

"Of course not, and I'm shocked you'd even suggest it."

"Oh. Well, see you around." He walked away.

"Good-bye, Ralph. I'll be heading back to the ranch. I appreciate your help and so forth, but I want the record to show . . ." He kept walking and I had to yell. "Ralph, I want the record to state that I don't approve of this dark side of your . . . What sort of naughtiness did you have in mind?"

"I'm gonna eat me a steak."

Huh?

At this point, we must bring this story to a close. What follows has been sealed and classified Top Secret. It won't be available to the general public for twenty-five years.

Sorry.

# CHAPTER SEVEN

# The Fling Begins

It's too bad we can't reveal any more about The Fling. It turned into quite an adventure, and I had several narrow escapes and close calls.

But we can't release any more details to the general public. You see, it contains certain . . . how can I say this without revealing too much? It contains certain information that could . . . uh . . . tarnish, shall we say, the reputations of several . . .

Might as well just blurt it out. Hang on, this might shock you.

See, I've always tried to be a good dog. No kidding. Since I was just a little shaver, I've tried to be a good dog and a good example to other dogs and little children. It's part of being a cowdog. It comes with the job of being Head of Ranch Security.

I have a reputation to protect. When the little children hear the name Hank the Cowdog, they naturally think of, well, courage and bravery, intelligence, good looks, dedication to duty, good looks, superior mental ability, and devilish good looks.

What they *never* think of when they hear my name is . . . well, naughty behavior. It's just not a part of my nature, and that's why I was so shocked and impaled when Ralph tried to lead me down the path of naughtiness.

Appalled, not impaled. Impaled means . . . I don't know what it means.

How foolish of him! How careless and insensitive! Why, the very idea . . . but you know, when he brought up the business of the steak . . . well, that kind of changed the deal.

I mean, what could be naughty about eating a steak? Steaks are wholesome and nourishing. Anything wholesome and nourishing can't possibly be unwholesome or unnourishing . . . or naughty. And that's when I knew, in my most secret heart of hearts, that Ralph was really a wonderful guy and a model of good behavior. Yes, he was a little boring, and yes, he was just a jailhouse mutt, but down deep, he was the kind of dog you'd want your kids to own and play with.

And I realized that he was the kind of dog I,

uh, needed to associate with—because of his immuckable standards of conduct and because of his passionate interest in . . . well, nutrition and wholesome dietary so forths.

And besides that, he needed a friend to keep him out of trouble, just in case things got out of control on The Fling. I knew he would be safe with the Head of Ranch Security, so you see, there was a Higher Motive in my decision to . . .

This is going so well that we might declassify the rest of the story. What do you think? Should we risk it?

Tell you what, if you'll promise to ignore any parts of the story that might, uh, cast doubts on my reputation, we might risk letting you take a peek. But you have to promise.

Okay. The Fling began innocently enough, with Ralph saying something about food . . . steak, actually, and you know where I stand on the issue of steak. I'm 100 percent in favor of steaks. I love 'em and have very few opportunities to eat 'em.

They don't often feed us steak at the ranch, you know. The people there are kind of cheap. Oh, they'll sure feed steak to guests who come in for a few hours' visit, but do you think they'll waste a steak on their own Head of Ranch Security, the guy who's out there in the dark protecting their ranch? Oh no. That would cost too much and drive the whole operation into bankrubble.

So they give us Co-op dog food—tasteless dry kernels of . . . something. Sawdust, perhaps, and stale grease. Is that fair? Is that just? No, it's not fair at all, but I can't allow myself to get worked up over the injustice in the world, so let's just skip it. I'll say no more about it.

Yes I will. I want the record to show that my lust for beefsteak was caused by the owners of my ranch, and their stingy, penny-pinching No Steak Policy toward dogs. If it hadn't been for that, I would never have been lured into The Fling.

Off we went on our little romp through town. I, being a trusting soul, followed my pal Ralph down the street. He was in high spirits.

That seems odd, doesn't it? A basset hound in high spirits. I mean, they always look so sad and mournful, but old Ralph was actually wearing a grin. This business of The Fling appeared to be a big deal to him. After spending months cooped up at the pound, he was now loose in the world. We were both in high spirits, and it seemed a perfect time to knock out a little song about our adventure. Would you like to hear it? Here's how it went.

## The Fling Song

*Hank*
Hey, Ralph, I've got a question I must pose.
    (I must pose)
Before today, I would describe you as morose.
    (Mo-rose)
And maybe just a little boring
Now I see your mood is soaring,
I don't get it, pal, you're blooming like a rose.
    (Like a rose)

*Ralph*
Well, I'm here to tell you something 'bout a
    hound, ('bout a hound)
Even one who makes his living in the pound.
    (In the pound)
You may think my life is wretched
Just because my face suggests it,
But that changes when old Ralphie hits the
    town. (Hits the town)

On a fling (on a fling), on a fling
    (on a fling)
You can do almost anything.
If you have a naughty thought
Or some act you shouldn't ought,

**68**

The time to do it's when you go out
   on a fling.

*Hank*

I'll be derned, Ralph, this is sounding
   interesting. (Interesting)
And I think I just might get into the swing.
   (In the swing)
Eating steak sounds mighty fine,
I just wonder who is buyin'.
Or is everything provided on a fling?
   (On a fling)

*Ralph*

Yup, you bet, them yummy steaks are
   free and clear. (Free and clear)
People cook 'em and we suddenly appear.
   (Appear)
You might say it's just a service,
There's no need for being nervous,
Now it's time for us to get our tails in gear.
   (Tails in gear)

   On a fling (on a fling), on a fling
      (on a fling),
   You can do almost anything.
   If you have a naughty thought

Or some act you shouldn't ought,
The time to do it's when you go out
on a fling.

Pretty neat song, huh? You bet. Well, we made our way down a street lined with nice houses and neat yards. We had gone a couple of blocks when we heard a vehicle approaching from the east. Ralph stopped and gave me a wink.

"That'll be Jimmy Joe. We'd better hide."

We took cover in some shrubs and waited. Sure enough, a white pickup with a cage in the back came creeping down the street. As it drew closer, I could see that it was driven by none other than Jimmy Joe Dogcatcher. His eyes were prowling the yards on both sides of the street.

He drove past us and I dared to grab a breath of air. Whew! But then he stopped. He got out of the cab, carrying his rope in his left hand. I pressed myself deeper into the shrubberies and held my breath again.

He spoke. "Ralph, I know you're out there. I've already got a complaint on you for standing in the middle of the street. You've had your fun. Come on in. Here, Ralphie! Here, boy!" He cocked his ear and listened. Then his eyes swung around and focused on the very bush where we were hid-

ing. "Come on, Ralphie, give it up, son."

Well, I figured that was the end of The Fling. We'd been caught. I turned a questioning gaze on Ralph. He shook his head and whispered, "He's bluffing. If he'd seen us, he wouldn't have said anything. He's a crafty old coot."

Sure enough, Jimmy Joe's eyes moved away from our bush and scanned the other yards on the block. Then he grinned, pitched a heeling loop at the left rear tire of the pickup, coiled up his rope, got in, and went creeping on down the street.

As the hum of his motor disappeared in the distance, we raised our heads out of the shrubberies. Ralph was grinning.

"Huh, huh. We done him good on that one."

"So . . . this is just a game you guys play?"

"Yup. He enjoys it as much as I do, only he can't come right out and say so—him being the dog-catcher and everything."

"Now wait a minute. He was looking for you just now, but he didn't want to catch you? Is that what you're saying?"

"Uh-huh. That'd be too easy. We both kind of like to string it out, don't you know. Gives us something to do."

"I see. Well, this is pretty strange, Ralph, but I must admit . . . uh, what was it you said a while ago? Something about eating a steak?"

He glanced up and down the street, then started walking. "Yup. That's the good part. You'll like it."

"I'm sure I will. I'm very fond of steak, you know, but . . . tell me again where it comes from."

"Steak's provided by the townfolks."

"No kidding? Gee, that's nice of them. I guess the whole town's in on this, huh?"

"Something like that."

I didn't ask any more about it. Maybe I should have.

We continued walking down the sidewalk, and I began to notice that Ralph had his nose up in the air and was sniffing. I took this as a cue and followed his lead. Minutes passed. We came to the end of the block and crossed the street. He was still sniffing the air.

"Ralph, I notice that we're sniffing."

"Uh-huh."

"Are we sniffing for anything in particular or . . . just sniffing?"

"Uh-huh."

"Okay, maybe you want me to guess, huh? Let's see here." I drew in a large sample of atmospheric particles and began analyzing them. "I'm picking up traces of . . . two dogs."

"Nope."

"I'm picking up tiny traces of . . . Hey Ralph, I can't smell much of anything, to tell you the truth, so maybe you could . . ."

Just then he stopped walking. His sniffing increased and his head moved slowly to the left. "There we go. Bingo. That yard over yonder."

My gaze went to the yard directly across the street from us. I studied it carefully, memorizing every detail. "What's in the yard that we smell, Ralph? The bicycle?"

"Nope."

"The car?"

His eyes came around and locked on me. "You know, you'd have more fun if you let me handle this."

"Fine. Sorry. I was just trying to help."

"Uh-huh, only your nose works about as good as a big rock."

"Well, I'm not so sure about that. For your information, the lady dogs go nuts over my nose. I've been told it's a refined nose, handsome and dignified."

"Uh-huh, and if it was a gun, you'd be shooting blanks. You don't smell that steak?"

I drew in a big gulp of atmospheric particles. "I . . . no. Do you?"

"Sure. I can even tell you how many steaks. Four."

I was impressed. "You can smell all that from across the street? That's amazing."

He gave me a wink. "I'm a hound. Hounds wrote the book on smells. You ready to eat?"

"Well, I . . ." He had already started across the street. I trotted after him. "You mean, these people are just . . . donating the steaks to us?"

"Something like that. Just foller me and don't mess up."

And so it was that I followed Ralph into . . .

Trouble.

# CHAPTER EIGHT

# Our Secret Mission into the Yard

**B**y the time we reached the front yard, I had caught the scent. "Hey Ralph, I can smell it now. Barbecue. An outdoor cooker, right?"

His eyes swung around and he gave me a sour look. "It might be all right if you want to quit asking questions."

"Hey, I was just trying to make conversation."

"Uh-huh, but we're coming to the tricky part, so maybe you could hush."

"Well gee, sorry, but I must tell you, Ralph, that I don't appreciate your suggestion that I'm a blabbermouth. Nothing could be further from the truth. In actuality . . ."

"Are you gonna hush or are you gonna yap?"

"I'm going to . . . hush."

"Good. Foller me."

I decided to let it drop, but I didn't forget it. The very idea, him suggesting that I talked too much! It caused a deep wound in my . . . whatever, and I decided then and there that Ralph wasn't the nice guy I'd thought he was.

Telling me to shut up. I'd never been so insulted. By a hound dog, anyway. Oh well.

We passed through the front yard and crept around the side of the house. We came to a wooden fence. Ralph pointed to it with his nose.

"Can you dig?"

"Sure I can dig. I'm a ranch dog, remember? We're . . ."

"Then dig."

"Are you sure it's okay? I mean, some people don't approve . . ."

He heaved a sigh and rolled his eyes. "You want me to do it?"

"No, I don't want you to do it. I'm perfectly capable of digging, but digging up yards can get a dog in trouble. I know these things, trust me."

"Dig."

"Okay, I'll dig." I moved into position and began excavating a tunnel under the fence. "There, I'm digging. You see? But while I'm digging, I want to . . ."

He covered his ears with his paws. Fine. If he insisted on being so rude, such a cad, I didn't want to talk to him anyway. I threw myself into the digging process, clawing up huge gobs of dirt and flinging them into the air, and, heh heh, somehow the dirt went in Ralph's direction and sprayed him good.

"Reckon you could point that dirt somewheres else?"

"No. And don't talk while I'm working. That's the trouble with you, Ralph, you're a blabbermouth. How can I dig a hole with all your jabbering?"

That got him, and he deserved it too.

Well, it didn't take me long to build a nice tunnel under the fence. I stepped back and gave him a triumphant smile. "You wanted a hole, there's a hole. Now what?"

He shook the dirt off his face and waddled over to the hole. "I'll get the steaks. You wait here."

I found myself studying him with narrowed eyes. "What are you saying, Ralph? You think I'm not qualified to enter the yard? Or maybe it's something else. How do I know you'll come back with the steaks, huh? You've got a prison record, you know."

He rolled his eyes. "Let's go. Just don't mess up."

"Mess up, ha! Listen, bud, you happen to be talking to the Head of . . ."

He wasn't listening. He stepped down into the hole and wiggled his way through. I did the same, and we came out on the other side.

"... Ranch Security."

"Will you hush?"

We came up in a backyard. I guess that was obvious, but it wasn't so obvious that it had a cement patio, several fruit trees, and a barbecue cooker. It was hissing and smoking—the cooker was—and now I was getting a strong reading of... *meat*. I scanned the entire yard and committed it to memory. A guy never knows when some tiny detail might turn out to be...

HUH?

A dog? A huge black dog? Yipes, there was a huge black Labrador sleeping beside the cooker! I shot a glance at Ralph. He had spotted the dog and his eyes showed concern. And that's when I began to wonder if there was more to this deal than I'd been told.

I dropped my voice to a whisper. "Ralph, are you sure..."

He waved me off, as if to say, "Don't worry, everything's fine."

Ha. I should have known. When you tunnel into a yard with a big black dog, everything isn't fine.

Just then the back door opened, and out walked

a man. Description: I don't remember, he was just a man. Oh, he was carrying a plate in one hand and some tongues in the other. Tongs. Pinchers. What do you call those things? Never mind.

He walked to the cooker and lifted the lid. Smoke billowed out and filled the air with . . . My mouth began to water. That was the smell of steak, no question about it, and probably sirloin, my very favorite kind.

Well, my very favorite after T-bones, but what the heck. When the nice people of Twitchell go to the trouble to fix you a sirloin steak, you don't wish for T-bones. You take what's offered.

What a nice guy he was, fixing steak for me and Ralph. They must have been friends or something.

The man fussed over the meat, pushed it around on the grill. Then he lifted out several hunks and set them on the plate. He went back into the house. The Labrador lifted his head and looked around. I noticed that Ralph flattened himself out on the ground.

"Hey Ralph," I whispered, "what's the deal here? You don't know that dog?"

He held his paw up to his lips and told me to shhhh.

The Lab swept the yard with his eyes and went back to sleep. Ralph slowly pushed himself up to a standing position and gave me a wink. He started creeping over to the cooker. Suddenly I remembered that when he walked, his claws clicked . . . whew, but that was only on hard surfaces such as pavement, and he was walking through grass.

So far so good. He reached the cooker, and the black dog was still sleeping. Just a little farther. To snag the meat, Ralph would have to go up on his hind legs and get his mouth over the top of the plate.

*Go on, Ralph, hop up.*

He hopped up on his back legs . . .

*Good, good, keep going.*

He balanced his weight on his back legs . . .

*Now push yourself up.*

He pushed himself up and . . . tumbled over backward! He made a swishing sound in the grass. The black dog's ears twitched. One eye drifted open. I thought he was going to wake up, but he didn't. Whew! We had dodged a bulletin.

A bullet, shall we say. We had dodged a bullet.

Ralph pushed himself up to a standing position and glanced back at the house. He was going to try it again, but he would have to hurry. The meat on the grill was hissing and smoking. Soon it would be done and the man would be back for it.

Ralph crouched down and threw his weight

upward . . . and he fell over backward again! What was the deal? This was turning into a comedy of arrows.

Errors, let us say, a comedy of errors.

My heart was pounding in my . . . well, in my chest, of course, and I could feel tingles of fear skating down my backbone. Suddenly it dawned on me that Ralph would never be able to reach the steaks. You know why? Because of the way his body was built.

See, your basset hounds have short legs and thick bodies. There are some things they can do well with such a body shape (I don't know what they are, come to think of it), but jumping up on their back legs isn't one of them.

If we wanted that meat, I would have to do the job.

I stepped forward and crept over to the cooker. I elbowed Ralph out of the way and dropped my voice to the faintest of whispers. "What kind of rookie deal is that? Get out of the way and I'll do it myself."

He didn't budge. "I can do it. Third time's a charm."

"Third time's a wreck, Ralph. You're too fat for this. Now move."

He edged out of the way. "Well, you'd better share the steaks."

"Of course I'll share the steaks. You said there were four of 'em. That's plenty for both of us. Now watch this and study your lessons."

As gracefully as a deer, as quietly as a jungle cat, I went up on my hind legs and peered over the edge of the . . .

Huh?

I eased myself back down and turned a steely glare on Ralph. "You said you smelled steaks, right? Four sirloin steaks?"

"I never said they were sirloins."

"Okay, but you said steaks. Well, they're not steaks, Ralph. It's a string of frankfurters, all tied together."

His ears jumped. "Weenies?"

"That's right, weenies, not steaks. I guess that nose of yours isn't so great."

"Well . . . it's meat. I kind of like weenies, how about you?"

I shot a glance at the black dog. He was still asleep and hadn't heard our whispering. "I like weenies, Ralph, but my heart was set on steak. This comes as a crushing disappointment."

"Uh-huh, but would you rather have weenies or be crushed?"

I cut my eyes from side to side. "It comes down to that, doesn't it? Okay, I'll settle for weenies,

Ralph, and I'll do the job for you, but we'll hear no more about your hotshot nose."

"Don't mess up."

I stuck my nose in his face. "Listen, bud, if I'd been in charge of this mission from the start, we'd have been in and out of here in nothing flat. I never mess up. I'm Head of Ranch Security, and I'm fixing to show you how it's supposed to be done."

I switched on the Hydraulic Lifting circuit and activated the enormous muscles in my hind legs. My body rose through the air—silently, flawlessly. You've seen huge hydraulic cranes and booms at work? Same deal. Pure power without even a whisper of noise.

The hydraulics worked to perfection, and within moments my nose and mouth were in position to make the snag. The important thing here was to execute the maneuver without disturbing the plate, see, snag the meat and leave the plate. If the plate fell off the cooker . . . well, that would be a rookie mistake and would get us in a bunch of . . .

The back door opened.

"Hey! Get away from my meat! Hyah! Scat!"

HUH?

"Margie, call the dogcatcher! There's a stray dog in our supper!"

Yipes!

# CHAPTER NINE

# Weenie Waves Cloud My Thinking

I should have known. Ralph had wasted precious time with all his fooling around, and now the cook had returned. We'd been caught in the act.

A huge decision loomed over me. Did we abort the mission . . . or should I grab the meat and hope for the best? My nose was positioned directly above the plate, and fragrant waves of steakness were . . . uh . . . clouding my judgment, shall we say, and . . .

Okay, they weren't Steak Waves. They were Weenie Waves, but those are some powerful waves and they made it hard for me to make a clear decision.

The man was yelling and coming down the steps. The Labrador's head came up and he was glaring at me with vicious green eyes . . . red eyes . . . he had eyes and they were glaring at me. I had to do something, and fast.

I grabbed the weenie string in my powerful jaws and headed for the tunnel. I can't be blamed for the broken plate. My plan had called for . . . We've already discussed my plan for the mission: in and out, no noise, no damage. But that had all gone by the hayseed when the chef had blundered out the door and started yelling.

Wayside. It had all gone by the wayside.

Anyway, the plate hit the cement patio and broke into a thousand pieces. By that time I had made the sprint across the yard and had reached the mouth of the tunnel. I know it was foolish of me, but instead of diving straight into the tunnel, I turned to check on my pardner.

I needn't have bothered. Ralph was not only right behind me, but he ran over me and pushed me away from the entrance. "Oops, sorry. Quick, give me the weenies."

"Are you nuts? Give you the . . ."

"Hurry! That dog's coming. You hold him off. You're better at security stuff than I am."

Well . . . that was true. My mind was racing. "Okay, Ralph, I'll have to trust you, but you'd better be waiting on the other side. If you run off with my meat, it will have a real bad effect on our relationship."

"No problem."

I gave him the weenie string. He seized it and dived into the escape tunnel. Then I whirled around to fight off . . . Good grief, I'd expected to see the dog charging me, but what was charging across the lawn and headed straight for me wasn't the dog.

*It was the man!* He had armed himself with a shovel and he was coming after me and, fellers, he looked MAD! Red face, bulging eyes, exposed fangs, and raised shovel.

Gulk.

Ralph's fat bohunkus was still plugging the tunnel, so I decided to try . . . well, charm and diplomacy. You shift all your circuits over to Sincerity and Remorse, and concentrate extra hard on beaming the "I didn't do it" message to the offended party. Sometimes it works.

And sometimes it doesn't.

BAM! Down came the shovel. It missed me by inches. I went to higher voltage on the Sincerity Transmission and . . .

BAM! If I just sat there, he was going to find his range with that shovel and do great harm to my body. At that point . . . BAM . . . we cancelled the

Sincerity Transmission and threw all circuits over to a setting we ... BAM ... call Rocket Dog.

I went to Turbo Six and took dead aim at the back fence. I had no choice but to batter my way through it. It looked pretty stout, probably five feet of solid wood, but there was a shovel-swinging lunatic behind me and I had to get out of there.

I felt the G-forces compressing the flesh of my

face. All my bodily fluids moved back into my tail section. Faster and faster. The earth was whizzing by me now, nothing but a blur. Fighting the terrible G-forces, I reached out and pushed the throttle one more notch—to Turbo Seven.

We had never traveled at this speed before. It was unknown territory. Would the equipment take it? Could our hardware stand such punishment? We just didn't know. We had simulated this contagency through Data Control, but that was simulation. This was the Real Thing.

I was aware that at any moment, my entire body might be vaporized in a violent explosion. A ball of fire, a column of smoke, and no one at the ranch would ever know what happened. They would grieve, mourn, cry, wear sackcloth and ashes for weeks and weeks, but they would never know how their heroic dog had met his end.

The fence loomed up before me. My mouth went dry. My lips were parched. Faster and faster. The moment was approaching. Five. Four. Three. Two . . .

I stepped in a stupid hole! Who would have expected . . . but at such astonishing speeds, even the tiniest of depressions on the launching surface can cause a derailment. This wasn't a tiny hole. It was a deep hole, probably dug by that idiot black dog, and suddenly everything went to pot and we found ourselves . . . well, doing cartwheels, you might say.

When I quit rolling, I was lying against the fence. BAM! There was the shovel again, and if I hadn't dodged, it might have changed the location of my head. Well, that was enough. It was time to sell the farm. Bail out. Abort the mission. I dashed between the man's legs while he was reloading the shovel, and crawled into a large bush.

It was dark in there. I could hear the man outside, muttering threats and thrashing on the bush.

"Come out of there, you thieving hound! Attila, get him! Tear him up!"

*Attila?* Who was . . . Oh yes, the big black dog. Gag, I had escaped one form of murder only to stumble into another. But where was he?

I cocked my ear and listened. I could hear him . . . breathing. He was in the bushes! Attila and I were occupying the same bush. It was an eerie sound, let me tell you, and what made it even spookier was that I couldn't see him. It's hard to see a black dog in the dark, right? That was the deal. I knew he was in there but . . .

I inched forward and . . . *bumped into something big and hairy.*

I froze. I didn't dare move or even breathe. I

cocked my ear and listened. The sound of his breathing had stopped. He had switched to Quick Quiet, just as I had, and we were now engaged in a very dangerous waiting game. The first one to breathe . . .

Silence. My whole body ached for air. I held my breath as long as I could. Then I took a gulp of air . . . and so did he. I heard it.

I swallowed hard. "Attila, I don't know you well. In fact, we've never been introduced, but we need to talk."

There was a throbbing moment of silence, then I heard his voice. "Right."

"I realize that from your perspective, this all looks pretty bad. I mean, a couple of strange dogs show up in your yard and . . . well, plunder the master's supper."

"Right."

"But I think I can explain everything. Will you listen, just for a moment? I'll be brief."

"Sure."

I breathed a sigh. "Great. Here's the straight story. You saw that other dog, right? Basset hound, short guy, big ears, sad eyes?"

"Right."

"He's a convicted murderer and he's been in jail for years. You ever visit the dog pound?"

"Not me."

"Well, that's where he's been until this afternoon. Attila, he broke out of prison this very afternoon and he's gone on a wild rampage. I tried to stop him but he . . . he threatened to tear me limb from shred."

"Oh my gosh!"

This was selling. I could tell by the tone of his voice. I plunged on.

"He came into this yard looking for a dog to eat."

"I knew it!"

"He saw you sleeping." I heard a gasp. "He was moving toward you." Another gasp. "But at the very last second, I smelled the meat cooking and said, 'Hey Killer, take the meat and leave the poor dog alone. Haven't you eaten enough dogs for one day?' And you know what he said?"

"Don't tell me, I don't want to know. Take the weenies, take the grill, take the whole yard, I don't care, but just get out of here."

"You really mean that? You're not sore about this?"

"Sore? Listen, fella, I ain't a guard dog. I play with tennis balls, know what I mean? They throw the ball, I chase it and bring it back. That's me, that's who I am. My whole life's wrapped up in chasing balls."

"So, if I happened to slither out of here, you, uh, wouldn't be bitter?"

"Right. Just leave. Look at me. I've got hives!"

"It's dark, I can't see."

"I've got hives. I can't stand the stress. Pressure kills me. Big bumps. They itch."

I began edging toward the tunnel. "Okay, Attila, have it your way. I'll leave."

"Great. Peace, brother."

"Same to you. And thanks for the weenies. You want us to save one for you?"

"Nah. Garlic gives me indigestion. Just go."

I shot out of the bushes. The man was standing right there with his shovel raised over his head. BAM! Did he think I was going to sit there and let him smash me? Ha. He could forget that. I put some amazing moves on him, juked him out of his shorts, and headed for the tunnel.

BAM! The foolish man thought he could run me down. Ha. I showed him speed like he'd never seen before. In a flash, I had streaked across the yard and dived into the tunnel and was heading for . . .

BAM!

. . . freedom, but my hiney was a little slow about getting under the fence and, yes, the insane person with the shovel finally scored a hit. It hurt pretty badly and gave me a slight tail concussion, but I managed to claw my way through the tunnel and popped out on the other side.

Wow, that had been a close one. I shook the dirt off my coat and was about to go looking for my treasure of captured weenies, but then I heard something that forced me to stop.

From the other side of the fence, I heard the man say, "Attila! Git 'im, boy! Tear 'im up!"

Then I heard the bushes crash. Then, barking at the top of his lungs, Attila hurled himself against the fence between us.

"Come back here, you dirty rat! I'll bust all your legs and tear off your ears! Where'd he go, let me at 'im!"

I thought about saying something to the mutt, but decided not to. What the heck, I had won the prize, and when you win, you can afford to be modest about it. Let him bark.

Besides, my mouth was watering and I could almost taste those barbecued weenies. I set out to find Ralph, never dreaming that . . . well, you'll see.

# CHAPTER TEN

# Ralph Stole My Weenie Feast, the Scrounge

Attila was a Labrador, right? And everybody knows that Labs are nothing but big cream puffs, right? What we had here was a yard mutt who was scared of his own shadow and played with tennis balls, so I felt pretty confident that . . .

The yard gate burst open and out stepped the former owner of the weenies. He was dragging Attila by the collar and pointing at . . . well, he sure seemed to be pointing at . . . ME.

"Git 'im, Attila! Do your stuff, boy!"

And here he came, bounding across the yard, and you know what? He didn't look like a cream puff any more. I saw a huge black body, blinking red eyes, and gleaming fangs, all coming straight at me.

My first reaction was to . . . well . . . to run. I mean, mostly I ran from the shock of it all, but also because . . . let's face it. Most people and dogs would run from a big black dog with blinking red eyes, right? They wouldn't just sit there and try to figure things out.

Yes sir, I ran and I wasn't ashamed to be running. But I also tried to conduct some Over the Shoulder Diplomacy.

"Hey, Attila, what's the deal here? I thought . . . Listen, bud, those hives are looking worse. No kidding. How about a few sets of tennis, huh? You go back to the house and find a ball and we'll . . ."

He was not only big, he was also quite a bit faster than you might have supposed. He closed the distance between us with those long loping strides and caught me just as I reached the middle of the street. He hit me with a full head of steam and sent me rolling.

When I quit rolling, he was right there in my face—all teeth and eyes and nastiness. I was lying on my back, which meant that my throat and belly were exposed to his fangs, if he chose to use them.

In a serious fighting situation, a guy never

wants to end up on his back. Have we mentioned that? It's true. Nothing could be worse. That's where I was, in the worst possible position to defend myself from this monster.

I looked into his blinking red neon eyes. They were heartless, showed no hint of mercy. But then . . . they sort of shorted out, you might say, and he spoke.

"Hey, fella, are you scared?"

"What?"

"Are you scared?"

"Uh . . . yes, I'm a little scared. How about you?"

"Out of my mind. I hate this stuff!"

"Yeah? Well, for a guy who hates violence, you're putting on a great show."

"That's all it is, nothing but a show. The boss wants it, know what I mean? I've got to do this to keep my job."

"Yeah? Well, maybe we can work out a deal."

He shot a glance back at the yard. His boss was standing there, waiting for some action. "Let's. You don't hurt me and I won't hurt you. We'll make it look good—growl, bite, snarl, roll around, lots of noise, big scene."

"Okay, that'll work."

"You lose the fight, see, and make me look good. You keep the weenies, I keep my job. Got it?"

"Got it. Uh . . . you'll have to let me up."

"Right, sure." He stepped back and I leaped to my feet. He gave me a wink. "You ready?"

"Sure. Let's go for it." I threw a wild punch and raised my voice. "There, take that, you ruffian rascal!"

"Good, good. Now here's mine. Watch this." He roared a bark and threw a wild punch. "There, take that, you shameless weenie thief!"

"Don't you call me a shameless weenie thief!"

"I'll call you a shameless weenie thief any time I want, because that's what you are!"

"Oh yeah? Well, you're nothing but a tennis-loving ruffian rascal with red eyes!"

He grinned and whispered, "Good shot, good

shot." Then he roared, "Don't you call me a tennis-loving ruffian rascal, you weenie-thieving shame-less cad!"

This went on for several rounds, and in between insults we threw a lot of punches that missed the mark. It was kind of fun, to tell you the truth, two dogs dancing around in the street, doing the things we had to do to keep our jobs and weenies.

Heh, heh. And Attila's boss, the dumbbell, ate it up. He was jumping up and down, yelling, and cheering us on to more and bloodier things. He must have thought this was a dogfight to the death. Heh, heh. Little did he know.

After several great rounds, I said, "What do you think? Enough?"

"Just a little more. I haven't seen the boss this happy in months."

"Okeydoke. Try this." I puffed myself up and yelled, "And furthermore, you big oaf, your mother's a fat cow!"

Attila stopped in his tracks and stared at me. "Why'd you say that?"

"Well, it's part of the show. You know, insults and stuff like that."

"Yeah, but . . . you insulted my momma."

"It was a joke. Hey, relax. I say that to the cat-tle at the ranch all the time."

"Yeah, but their mothers *are* cows. My momma's not a cow."

I rolled my eyes. "Don't I know that? Look, let's . . ."

He shook his head. His red-light eyes had come on again. "Uh-uh. You shouldn't have said that, man, you shouldn't have insulted my momma. I can't take that. It hurts too much."

"I don't believe this."

He advanced a step toward me. "It unleashes something terrible inside me."

I began backing up. "Attila, whoa, easy boy, settle down."

"I'm gonna wrap you around that light pole there, buddy, for telling lies about my momma."

"I take it back, okay? Your momma's a wonderful lady. She's not a fat cow. She's not fat. She's not even a cow."

"Too late, buddy, the damage is done."

Well, he was wrong about that. The damage *wasn't* already done, at least the damage to me, but he took care of that pretty quickly. We needn't dwell on the darker parts of the story. I'll say only that Attila lived up to his name, and he did try to wrap me around the light pole. The only reason he didn't get it done was that his aim was bad. Instead of hurling me into the light pole, he shanked his throw and put me into a rosebush instead.

After that, he didn't get another chance. I . . . uh . . . seized the opportunity to . . . uh . . . make a graceful exit. Okay, I ran, might as well come out and admit it, and he chased me for a whole block. No kidding, a whole block.

When he finally gave up the chase, he called out, "Hey, buddy, I'm sorry. I lost my head, know what I mean? Nothing personal, okay?"

Hunkered down in a flower patch, I yelled back—in the privacy of my own mind, that is—I yelled back, "Yeah, right, nothing personal. Well, your mother's still a fat cow and you're a lunatic! And see if I ever steal weenies from you again!"

There. That got him told. Peering out of the flowers and shrubberies, I saw him turn and leave, the coward, and go back to collect pats and congratulations from his boss. When he was a full block away, I raised up and yelled, "I guess you know this means war!"

He stopped and turned around. I ran.

Well, one of us had to show some maturity. I mean . . . skip it.

Having given the big lug the thrashing he so richly deserved, I went in search of my partner. Ralph. Remember Ralph? We'd pulled the job together, you might recall, and somewhere in this huge city, he was holding my share of the loot. I had to find him.

I walked down the street, calling his name. "Ralph? Oh, Ralph? Come out, come out, wherever you are. I'm ready to split the loot."

Weenies, oh boy. I could hardly wait.

I called and called, but Ralph was nowhere in sight. I walked down one side of the street, then crossed over and walked down the other. I saw some children playing. Several cars whizzed past. But no Ralph.

At that point I began to get suspicious. Surely my old pal didn't take off with all our loot. He wouldn't do that, would he? The more I thought about it, the more convinced I became that, yes, that's exactly what the scrounge had done.

I mean, he was a jailhouse mutt, right? Had a prison record as long as your leg. And what would a jailhouse mutt do if he found himself alone with a string of weenies? Stick around and wait for his partner to show up? Ha.

Oh, what a fool I'd been, trusting Ralph with my share of the business!

Bitter and angry thoughts marched across the parade ground of my mind. I had been swindled out of my fortune, and now I had nothing to show for my trip into town. We'd had our Fling, all right, and Ralph had flung me right into the garbage heap of Life.

He would pay for this. If I ever saw the mutt again, he would pay a terrible price for his greedy ways . . . but of course I would never get a chance to even the score. This was his town. No doubt he knew exactly how and where to disappear.

I had worked myself up into a towering fit of righteous anger and was walking past an alley, when I heard someone say, "Pssssst."

I stopped and turned my head slowly to the right, half expecting to see Attila, in which case I was primed and ready to, uh, take appropriate measures. Or could it be the dogcatcher? Yes, of course. Attila's master had told his wife to "call the dogcatcher," remember? I had forgotten about that, but now . . .

I was just about to set a Speed Course back to the ranch, when I saw a sad droopy basset face peering out from behind a garbage barrel. It was the face of a dog, and he seemed to be . . . calling me.

I squinted my eyes and studied the face. It looked a lot like Ralph's. Then he motioned me over with his paw.

I'll be derned, it was Ralph.

# CHAPTER ELEVEN

# Ralph's
# Tragic Story

When I recognized his face, I felt a huge sense of relief. My partner had been true to the end.

I dashed over to him and enveloped him in a big manly hug. "Ralph, by George, it's great to see you again! Where have you been? I looked everywhere."

"Well . . . I had a little trouble."

"Hey, you talk about trouble. When you left the yard . . ."

I told him the whole story about how I had fought my way out of the yard and was forced to give Attila the thrashing of his life. I could see that he was impressed.

"You done all that, huh? He was sure a big dog."

"He wasn't as big as he thought, Ralph, nor as

tough. If I could buy that mutt for what he's worth and sell him for what he *thinks* he's worth, I'd be a wealthy dog."

He chuckled. "Huh, huh. That's pretty good."

"You bet. Oh, it was a terrible fight, Ralph. We tore down a peach tree, knocked out a whole section of fence, hair flying, teeth flashing . . . wait a minute." I stopped and stared at the ground at Ralph's feet. "Where's the loot? Where are the weenies?"

Ralph hung his head. "Well . . . they're gone."

I held him in a blistering gaze. "Gone? Gone! I knew it, I knew you couldn't be trusted! Ralph, you've just broken my heart. I thought we were friends, pals, jailhouse buddies."

"They got stolen."

"I thought we were . . . What?"

"The weenies got stolen." His big sad eyes came up. "I waited for you across the street. While I was waiting, these two big dogs came along. They smelled the weenies and said they wanted 'em."

"Two big dogs . . . go on, Ralph, I want to hear the rest of this."

"Well, then they . . ." A big tear slid down his cheek and his lip trembled. "I can't go on. I'm ashamed of myself. You trusted me and I let you down."

He choked up and couldn't speak. I gave him a pat on the shoulder and began pacing in front of him. "It's all right, Ralph, just take it easy. Let me see if I can finish the story for you."

"Would you mind?"

"No problem. You see, Ralph, you've given me a couple of clues, and I can see the whole scene before my very eyes."

"Gosh. Really?"

"No kidding. It comes from years in the Security Business. You see, Ralph, in my line of work, we often start with tiny clues and reconstruct the entire crime. Let's see how close I can come." I set my jaw, lowered my brow, and plunged into deepest thought. "Okay, you're sitting there on the curb, waiting for me to return from combat."

"Yalp."

"You're sitting there, minding your own business, when these two big mutts pass by and catch a whiff of your weenies. *Our* weenies, actually."

"Uh-huh."

"Like I said, they're big guys, scruffy and hard-eyed and tough." I stopped pacing. "How am I doing so far?"

"Boy, you've nailed 'em."

I flashed a brief inward smile and resumed pacing. "This is just a hunch, Ralph, but let's throw it out. Their names were . . . Buster and Muggs."

He let out a gasp. "I'll be derned. How'd you know that?"

"I have my sources, Ralph, that's all I can tell you. We know about those guys and have been keeping files on them for a long time."

"Yeah, it was them, all right."

"Just as I suspected. Okay, they stop and they say . . . Buster would do the talking . . . Buster says, 'Say, pal, how would you like to share the weenies? We ain't had much to eat today.' Is that close?"

Ralph was amazed. "Boy yeah. That's just what he said, but how'd you . . ."

"Heh, heh. Years of experience with the crinimal mind, Ralph, but let me continue. It's coming fast now." I resumed pacing. "At first you try to ignore them, but they won't be ignored. You try to walk away with the weenies, but they block your path. By this time, you're getting scared."

"Yup. They were pretty scary guys."

"Just as I thought. Okay, at this point you're scared but you don't want to give up the weenies. I mean, we worked hard for those weenies and you don't want to lose them to a couple of bullies, so you . . . okay, you try to make a run for it. Am I right?"

His head bobbed up and down. "That's just

what I done. I tried to make a run for it."

"Right, and that's when they jumped you, Ralph. Those two big bullies jumped you and tore the string of weenies out of your mouth."

He was starting to cry again, as the painful memories returned. "Yes, yes! They tore the weenies right out of my mouth, the mean old things!"

I plunged on. "They stole the weenies from you, Ralph, and walked away . . . laughing."

"Yup, they laughed."

"Which left you feeling helpless and terrible, Ralph. See, you blamed yourself."

"Uh . . . yeah, I did, sure did."

"And those same feelings are coming back at this very moment, aren't they?"

"Yes!"

"And you're still blaming yourself, aren't you?"

"Yes! I'm a failure and a chicken liver! I should have gone down fighting!"

I paced over to him and patted him on the back. "I know how you must feel, Ralph, but I want you to know that our friendship is worth more than a string of weenies."

He looked at me through a veil of shimmering tears. "It is? You mean that?"

"Honest. We've been through so much . . ."

Suddenly, he burped. "Oops, 'scuse me."

"No problem. We've been through so much . . . Do you smell garlic?"

"Me? Nope, don't smell a thing."

"Hmm, that's odd. There for a second, I thought I smelled . . . Where was I?"

"In the yard with that big dog."

"Oh yes, there I was, facing this huge . . . We were talking about our relationship."

"Oh yeah." He burped again. "Sorry."

"No problem. Anyway, Ralph, the bottom line of all this is that you can't go on blaming yourself. Somehow you have to . . . I smell garlic again. You don't smell garlic?"

He sniffed the air. "Oh yeah, it's coming from the garbage barrel."

"Ah yes, of course. Somehow, Ralph, you have to pick up the pieces of your shattered life and move on."

He heaved a sigh. "Maybe you're right. Reckon I ought to go back to the dog pound?"

I gave that some thought. "Maybe you should. I mean, we had our Fling and it was a good experience for the most part."

"Yalp."

"We had some laughs and we had some tears, but what really matters, Ralph, is that it deepened our friendship. We lost the weenies, but by George, we have the memories."

"Yalp."

"And nobody can take those memories away from us, Ralph. They're precious and we'll keep them forever."

"I guess so." He pushed himself up. "Well, I'll be seeing you."

My gaze followed him. He was walking away. "Hey, wait a second. I wasn't quite finished."

"Uh-huh, but there's my ride."

It was then that I noticed the dogcatcher's pickup creeping down the street. Jimmy Joe was listening to country music on the radio and had his arm stuck out the window.

I followed Ralph into the street. "Hey, wait. We haven't even said good-bye."

"You might want to stay hidden. I'm Jimmy Joe's pet, but you're an escaped convict."

"Good point." I dived into a hedge. "Well, good-bye, old friend, old prison buddy. We had our Fling, didn't we?"

"Yalp. It was a good 'un. See you around."

"And don't blame yourself any more. It's just water under the dam."

He waved a paw in the air and went clicking out into the . . . He sure was walking funny. I mean, I hadn't noticed it before, but Ralph was *badly*

*overweight*. Why, he looked as though he had swallowed an inner tube or something.

He was as fat as a hog! He could barely walk on those short legs of his.

That happens to your town dogs, you know. They gulp down big meals and never get the proper exercise, and before you know it, they've taken on the shape of a weenie.

Oh well. Even though he was fat and not terribly smart, Ralph was my pal, and as I watched him waddle out to meet the dogcatcher, I felt a warm glow of satisfaction. We had shared some meaningful experiences and I had helped him through a deep personal crisis.

And now it was time for me to head back to the ranch—which, come to think of it, wasn't going to be such an easy matter. I mean, twenty-five miles across country . . . and it was getting dark.

Gulp.

I could only hope that the coyotes weren't out. If they were . . .

I waited for the dogcatcher to leave. When the sound of the pickup vanished into the distance, I pointed myself to the south and headed out in a long trot.

I would have to travel all night. With luck, I would be home by midmorning. Without luck, I would be . . . in trouble.

I made my way to the highway on the south edge of town and hit the road. Hours passed and the miles stretched out behind me. Darkness fell, and onward I plunged, driven by a powerful longing for my home. It suddenly occurred to me that I even missed . . . well, Drover.

It must have been around three o'clock in the

morning when I finally reached the Wolf Creek road. I was tired, but still had three miles to go. It seemed to me that I should stop and take a little . . .

Howling? I stopped and listened. There it was again, the howling of distant . . . coyotes, and all at once I felt refreshed and had no interest at all in stopping to rest. I needed to get home. Fast.

Have we discussed coyotes? Maybe not, but maybe we should. They can bark just like dogs. In many ways they look just like dogs. In other very important ways, they're not like dogs *at all*. In fact, they're dangerous to dogs.

They were close and getting closer. Good grief, I had walked right into the middle of a whole nest of cannibals! I could hear them barking and howling in all directions, which meant that . . . well, maybe I was surrounded. Yipes.

I happened to be standing at the base of a large cottonwood tree. Climbing trees wasn't part of my background or cultural heritage. I mean, that's the kind of thing cats do, but dogs? Never. As far as I knew, nobody in my family had ever climbed a tree or had even thought about climbing a tree.

Yet I was thinking very seriously about climbing this tree. Could it be done? Was it possible? The answer came to me in the form of a blood-chilling howl that errupted about a hundred feet in front of me. In a flash I leaped straight up, wrapped my paws around the first limb, and hauled my enormous body up into the tree.

You think dogs can't climb trees? Just bring in a few cannibals and see what happens.

But check this out. Suddenly I realized that the tree was full of . . . *big black things.*

# CHAPTER TWELVE

# Buzzards
# and Another
# Happy Ending

I sat down on a limb and glanced around. What were those large humps sitting on the limb beside me? I could just barely see them in the darkness, but I managed to count two of them. No, three. Four?

Holy cats, there was a whole line of these large dark forms perched on the limb! I cut my eyes from side to side. What was going on here? After a moment of deep thought, I dared to reach out a paw and touch . . . and suddenly I heard a voice. It said:

"Hee hee hee. Th-th-that t-t-tickles. Are y-y-you a b-buzzard?"

To which I said, "Why . . . yes, of course. Yes, I am definitely a buzzard. How about yourself?"

"Oh y-y-yeah, I've b-b-been a b-buzzard m-m-most of my l-life."

"Same here. It's a great way to, uh, make a living, isn't it? And a good wholesome lifestyle, I guess you'd say."

"Oh y-y-yes, w-w-we're very p-p-proud, m-m-me and Pa. H-have you m-m-met my p-p-pa?"

Wait, I recognized that voice. It was Junior. Quickly, I tried to cover for myself.

"No, I don't think we've met. I'm, uh, new here, just flew in from Abilene."

"You w-w-want to m-meet my p-p-pa? I c-c-can w-w-w-wake him up."

Just then, a loud hacksaw voice cut through the silence. "You already did, Junior, so y'all don't need to whisper and tippy-toe, 'cause you've already woke up me and half the buzzards in the Panhandle."

"Oh g-g-g-good."

"What's good about it? Sleeping is good, son. Wakin' up is the pits. I did a hard day's work today and when I come home to the roost, I expect to sleep, not listen to a bunch of chatterboxes talkin' about nuthin' and wakin' up the whole tree."

"P-p-p-pa?"

"What!"

"I w-w-want to introduce y-y-you to my n-n-new f-f-friend, new friend."

Have you figured it out? I had climbed up into a tree that happened to be the local buzzard roost, and it appeared that there were dozens of 'em. Buzzards, that is. The tree was full of big black sleeping buzzards—including Wallace and Junior. Pretty scary, huh?

Well, Wallace leaned forward and looked at me. In the pale moonlight of the moon, I saw just enough of him to get a description: Ugly. Very ugly.

He spoke. "Name's Wallace."

"Okay. Hi, Wallace. How's life?"

"Life's hard. That's why we sleep at night."

"H-h-h-he's from Abilene, P-p-pa."

"Huh. Don't they believe in sleepin' down there? And I'll tell you something else, Junior. He looks like some kind of freak to me."

"P-p-pa, h-h-hush."

"Well? It's true, ain't it?"

"H-h-h-he's d-different, is all."

Wallace leaned forward again and scowled at me. "That's the only buzzard I ever seen with ears."

"W-w-well, that's j-j-just the w-way they d-d-dress down at Abilene."

"That ain't dress, son, that's equipment. Show

me a buzzard with ears and I'll show you . . ." All at once Wallace looked down at the ground below. "Junior, son, I don't want to scare you, but there's somebody down at the base of this tree. Reckon you ought to swoop down there and check it out?"

Junior rocked forward and looked down. "Uh . . . n-n-no, I d-d-don't think so."

"Who do you reckon they are?"

"W-w-well, I'd s-s-say m-m-maybe th-they're c-c-c-coyotes."

There was a long moment of silence, and in the silence we could hear sounds drifting up from below: the tramping of feet, the low rumble of voices, and an occasional burst of harsh laughter. I got the feeling that Wallace was staring at me.

"Hey, you with the ears. Abilene. How would you like to go down there and tell them rowdies to shove off and take their noise to some other tree? 'Cause if you don't, we're liable to be up all night, and I've got a big day tomorrow."

At that very moment our conversation was interrupted by a loud voice from down below, and I must admit that it sent a cold chill through my entire body.

"Uh! Coyote get strong smell of dog, follow strong smell to tree. Coyote think dog hiding up in treetop."

Wallace and Junior exchanged worried glances. Then Wallace whispered, "Son, we have barbarians at the gate." The old man glared down at the coyotes. "Now y'all boys better knock off the noise and go on home, we're trying to sleep up here."

"Ha! Coyote not give a hoot for sleep, want dog from treetop."

"We ain't got a dog. Dogs don't live in trees, and if y'all keep on making all that racket, you're fixing to learn something about buzzards you really don't want to know."

This was greeted with a chorus of hooting and laughing, and all at once the tree began to shake. Bam, bam, bam! It appeared that the coyotes were head-butting the tree, if you can believe that, which gives you some idea of just how tough those guys were.

Then we heard the voice again. "Coyote get tired and tiredest of waiting, maybe tear down whole tree and find dog for eat!"

Wallace puffed himself up. "Hoss, I'm runnin' out of nice ways of tellin' y'all to scram out of here." Bam, bam! Wallace heaved a sigh and shook his head. "Okay, y'all have asked for it and begged for it, so you're fixin' to get it."

You know what he did? He leaned out over the limb and proceeded to *throw up* on the cannibals.

That's what buzzards do when they get mad, don't you know, and it's . . . We don't need to go into chilling details about the, uh, molecular structure of what went down on top of their heads. It was too awful to describe.

Fellers, you talk about something that will kill a party. That did it. A moment of eerie silence followed, as poisonous fumes and vapors spread through the airwaves. Then . . . an explosion of screams and shouts, the crashing of brush, and the thunder of footsteps fading into the night. Then . . . silence.

Wallace sniffed his nose and rubbed his belly. "Dadgum rowdies. That was the best skunk I'd eaten in months." He turned to us. "Well, you reckon we can get some sleep now?" He fanned the air with his wing. "Shew! Them coyotes need to take a bath once in a while. Night, y'all."

"N-n-n-night, P-p-pa, and n-n-nice w-w-work, nice work."

I didn't say a word. I was having trouble just breathing. I didn't figure I'd ever get to sleep, and if I ever did, I was pretty sure I'd end up falling out of the tree. But somehow it all worked out, and the next thing I knew it was dawn.

What woke me up was the sound of singing. I know, that sounds odd, but when my eyes popped open, I found myself looking at one of the most peculiar scenes you can imagine: a whole tree-full of big black birds, all singing the same chant in unison. It went like this.

## Buzzard Chant

Morning sun and morning light,
Fading stars and fading night.
Diamond dew frosts sparkling grass,
Yellow sun rays have come at last.

Warm's the sun and still's the air,
Gone's the darkness everywhere.
Hills in purple shadows sprawl,
Haze and fogginess cover all.

Thanks we give for peaceful sleep,
For a day in which to reap,
Crystal air and endless sky,
And for the wings that let us fly.

Spread we now our feathered wings,
Soaring soft and silent rings.
May this day bring us success
Finding a cure for hungriness.

Pretty strange, huh? I thought so, and when they finished the song, they all spread their big black wings, pushed off their respective limbs, and soared off into the morning sky, until there were only three of us left in the tree: me, Wallace, and Junior.

I began to realize that Wallace was glaring at me. Let me tell you, that's a bad way to start the morning, with a buzzard glaring at you.

"Junior, wake up and look at your so-called friend. You said he was a buzzard from Abilene? Just happened to be wearin' a pair of ears? Ha. Wake up and you'll see what I tried to tell you last night but you wouldn't listen, and never do."

Junior yawned and blinked his eyes at me. "Oh m-my g-g-goodness, it's our d-d-doggie friend, doggie friend!"

I gave him a nod. "Morning, Junior."

"W-w-well, D-d-d-doggie, w-w-we have to g-g-go to w-w-work, go to work, and h-h-hunt some g-g-grub."

"Well, glory be!" Wallace muttered. "I'd begun to wonder if you'd planned to order in a pizza. Let's get airborne, son, we're already behind."

Wallace spread his wings and flapped away. Junior smiled, waved the tip-end of his wing, and flew away, leaving me all alone in the tree.

I jumped to the ground and trotted the last three miles to ranch headquarters. I was feeling pretty good about things. It was a beautiful morning. I had managed to dodge the cannibals and survive another night. And we mustn't forget that I'd had a Big Fling in town and had even managed to pull my friend Ralph through a deep personal . . .

Wait a second, hold everything. Remember that story Ralph told me, about how the two bullies stole the weenies from him? Well, in the middle of the night, I woke up and realized that my restless mind had been working on that very case, even as my body got some well-deserved slumber. The pieces of the puzzle suddenly fell into place, and you just won't believe what I figured out. Here, look at the evidence.

Evidence #1: Ralph burped, remember? And I smelled garlic.

Evidence #2: He burped again, and I smelled garlic again.

Evidence #3: Weenies are known to contain a lot of garlic.

Evidence #4: When Ralph walked away, I noted that he was fat and *shaped like a weenie*.

Do you see it now? You missed it the first time around, didn't you? Well, he didn't fool me, not for a . . . okay, he fooled me. *The scrounge ate all my weenies,* and I believed his silly, outrageous, unbelievable story!

But the important thing here was that I had learned a valuable Lesson on Life: Never trust your lunch with a jailhouse mutt. That had made the whole experience . . . phooey.

Case closed.

See you down the road.

# Have you read all
# of Hank's adventures?

☐ Yes, I want to join Hank's Security Force. Enclosed is $11.95 ($8.95 + $3.00 for shipping and handling) for my **two-year membership**. [Make check payable to Maverick Books.]

**Which book would you like to receive in your Welcome Package? Choose any book in the series.**

**(#      )      (#      )**
FIRST CHOICE          SECOND CHOICE

_____ **BOY or GIRL**
YOUR NAME                                (CIRCLE ONE)

_____
MAILING ADDRESS

_____
CITY                          STATE    ZIP

_____
TELEPHONE                     BIRTH DATE

_____
E-MAIL

Are you a ☐ Teacher or ☐ Librarian?

**Send check or money order for $11.95 to:**

Hank's Security Force
Maverick Books
P.O. Box 549
Perryton, Texas 79070

**DO NOT SEND CASH. NO CREDIT CARDS ACCEPTED.**
_Allow 4–6 weeks for delivery._

_The Hank the Cowdog Security Force, the Welcome Package, and_ The Hank Times _are the sole responsibility of Maverick Books. They are not organized, sponsored, or endorsed by Penguin Putnam Inc., Puffin Books, Viking Children's Books, or their subsidiaries or affiliates._